# MATILDA PLUM STARTER COLLECTION

CONNOR WHITELEY

# DEDICATION

Thank you to all my readers without you I couldn't do what I love.

# INTRODUCTION

Time to step away from mystery and science fiction short stories, and we need to look at one of my favourite genres of all time, the fantasy genre.

Personally, I've always loved how the fantasy genre is massive in scope but there are common elements in all the different stories. I love the magic and the sense of awe that the genre gives me, because fantasy stories are meant to be escapism, fun and positive with the good guys always winning.

Those are the reasons why the fantasy genre is brilliant in my opinion.

Therefore, I have a lot of different fantasy series from my Fireheart Fantasy Series, my Winter Fantasy Series, Rising Realm series, Cato Fantasy Series and on and on and on.

I love my fantasy fiction.

On the other hand, and this is a hot take I know, but I seriously do not like superheroes. I don't like Marvel, I don't like DC and I don't like the concepts of superheroes but somehow I ended up writing a superhero series.

Which I seriously enjoy.

As a result, this volume focuses on a fun, light-hearted and stellar fantasy series that I flat out love. It is my *Matilda Plum Fantasy Stories*, which I cannot get enough of because they are always fun, they are always weird and they are pure escapism for me.

As you'll expect by volume 4 in this series, you'll get to enjoy twenty gripping, enthralling fantasy short stories exploring all the weird, wonderful and surprising adventures that Matilda Plum finds herself in.

And I really like Matilda Plum because I'm a psychology graduate and I'm hoping to be a clinical psychologist in the future (just think mental health or therapist), and there are so many annoying myths and misconceptions around psychologists.

One day, I just sat down to write and I must have been so annoyed at a particular myth or misconception that I ended up writing about a character that had superpowers coming from these myths and misconceptions.

That is how Matilda Plum was born and I've loved writing her ever since.

In addition, I think there are certain fiction inspirations too, because Dean Wesley Smith has two great series that I highly recommend and enjoy. His Marble Grant series is a lot of fun as are his Poker Boy stories. They might have inspired this series a little bit but this series was mainly one born out of annoyance because people just believe these myths and misconceptions about psychologists without a second thought.

This is a really fun series though.

And if you like this series then you can find all the novellas and other short stories of the series on all major eBook retailers, you can order the paperback and hardback from online retailers and your local bookstore and library if you request it. As well as you can find an audiobook version narrated by artificial intelligence for the books at selected audiobook retailers.

Or just head on over to https://www.connorwhiteleyfiction.com/matilda-plum-superhero-fantasy-series

So now we know more about this enthralling series, let's turn over the page and start reading some stellar stories.

## CAPACITY TO CHANGE

As I leant against the cold brick wall of one of the many little shops in Canterbury high street with its cobblestone ground, little cafes everywhere and plenty of university students, I just watched people go about their business in the busy university city.

The air was amazingly fresh with the hints of pine, designer coffee from the local coffee shops and the strange combination of all the wonderful brands of aftershave and perfumes the students wore. That all combined to leave a strange, but rather pleasant, taste of refreshing mint on my tongue.

I always had loved Canterbury that little historic city in the south of England that no one actually cared about, remembered or did too much with. But I had gone to university, lost my virginity here too and just fell in love with the city.

So when I became a superhero in the counselling and therapy sector, I knew exactly where I wanted to return to. I had to come back to the place I love, and with there being three universities close by, I just knew that there would never be a shortage of people who needed my help.

It really just makes me smile now, because before I became a superhero I was a mental health doctor and worked for the National Health Service, but the amount of myths and stigma and other awful things I faced on a daily basis was ridiculous.

All because people believed psychology wasn't a real science and therapy was useless, and I was only good at profiling people.

Hell! Psychology isn't profiling. Profiling is shit.

But I really do laugh at it all now, because it turned out that a bunch of my superhero powers are versions of the psychology myths. And they are pretty cool. I can know everything about a person just by what they say, I can read their minds and I can influence them if I really want to.

Being a superhero is great!

So that was what I was doing today, I was simply walking around Canterbury wanting to find someone who needed my help. Of course, I always hoped when I went out that I wouldn't find anyone. I always had hated seeing people in pain.

But there were always people needing my help.

As all the young university students laughed and talked and listened to the street musicians, I couldn't help but start to feel like something was off ever so slightly.

I focused on all the people walking up and down the high street and noticed that one particular man in the crowd was giving off a slightly red aura.

That was definitely still a superpower I was getting used to, seeing people's auras was still so strange to me, but I was sure that this person was in deep trouble.

I slowly started to glide through the crowd towards him and I just stopped. A few people bumped into me and started to look annoyed but I just focused on my smile and that seemed to make them happy, so they went on with their day.

I stepped back out of the crowd so I wouldn't bump into anyone else, and I was right. I recognised that particular man with his middle-aged fit body, long black beard and expensive look. He was another superhero, yes, he worked in the Gambling Sector.

I couldn't remember for the life of me what his name was, but I had worked with him decades ago on helping a young woman off her gambling addiction. But I couldn't understand why this man wasn't okay.

And the red aura was still troubling.

Normally when people were sad, annoyed or depressed they just looked it and my superpowers would direct me in their direction. There was none of this red aura stuff.

So why was he giving off a red aura and what did it mean?

With me being a relatively new superhero (at least when compared to those who had been one since ancient times), I just knew that I was going to need help, superhero help.

"Octavia!" I shouted.

A few people looked at me weirdly and I quickly realised that I had to stop doing that in public.

But a few moments later everyone around me sort of became blurry and then one of the most stunning women I had ever seen just appeared, and everyone in the high street just acted like she had always been there.

Now I was definitely into both men and women, and whilst I seriously leant more towards men most of the time, Octavia was definitely one of those women that made me question myself. She was that stunning.

I had always loved her stunningly fit body without an ouch of body fat, her long wavy brown hair and just her smile. Believe me that smile could honestly melt the icecaps without any help from global warming.

So yea, she really was that stunning, and damn well hot.

"Matilda darling," Octavia said with a massive smile.

Octavia was probably the first ever superhero I met decades ago during my own transformation into a full superhero. She had worked in a few different sectors of the superhero world, and now I knew she was currently working in the Gambling Sector and helped out there.

If anyone would know what was going on with that red aura man it would be Octavia. So I just pointed to him, and Octavia's face just dropped.

"Well my darling that is hardly a good aura," Octavia said. "I had heard a rumour he was bad..."

Then Octavia just started to look me up and down and smiled. God, that smile could make me do anything.

"Matilda darling, are you free for a little helping?" Octavia asked.

I just smiled. "What's going on?"

Octavia gestured us to glide into the crowd and walk with everyone else as we spoke, but I knew she wanted to stay close to the red aura man. I just didn't know why.

"His name is Jaxon Ellis. A Superhero in the Gambling sector, a very good one from what I heard but he has a problem...,"

I just shook my head. Saying that people had problems was so horrible, demeaning and so last century. Modern day mental health preferred to describe that as difficulties, since these "problems" were just a part of a person, but they should be changed to help them have less "problematic" behaviour.

But I decided this wasn't the time for details with sexy Octavia.

"Is that why you started working with the Gambling Sector?" I asked.

Octavia nodded. "Yes Jaxon went missing, superhero worked needed to be done so I stepped up,"

"What is his difficulty?" I asked.

A few people bumped into us and knocked Octavia into my arms, that was a very pleasurable accident. She quickly stood up and got back to walking with the crowd.

Shame.

"He has what professional gamblers call a leak,"

I bit my lip and nodded. I had treated plenty of gambling addicts over the decades in my practice and I had come to understand that there was real skill involved in poker, and you could actually win a lot of money playing it.

Yet you were stupid to try and play and win at blackjack, the slot machines and the other games in casinos where the house would rig the odds in its favour. That's why professional gamblers never played those sorts of games.

Clearly Jaxon wasn't as professional as I thought, and it was clearly affecting his mental health.

"How much has he lost?" I asked.

"He's homeless. His kids and parents and wife won't talk to him and he is about to be fired as a superhero,"

I just stopped dead in my tracks. Lots of people bumped into and swore but I used my calming superpowers to make them happy.

I pulled Octavia against a window of a small supermarket near the edge of the high street.

Before now I didn't know that could actually happen, superheroes were superheroes. I didn't think we could get fired or anything.

"How do I help him?" I asked.

Octavia frowned. Damn even with her frowning she was hot as hell.

"He is another one of your… clients as you like to call them. Treat him and see if he wants to get better. Then call me with your results,"

With that everyone round me became blurry once more and then Octavia was gone. I always liked it how easy and straight forward people made therapy sound, but even as a superhero it still took time.

I looked back into the crowd of people and saw Jaxon was lighting a cigarette and walking towards me. His red aura started to get bigger and bigger and darker.

Then as he stood next to me I instantly recognised the smell as weed. He wasn't just smoking a cigarette, he was trying to get stoned.

I went over to him and gently tapped his shoulder.

I didn't always need people to talk to me to be able to analyse them and see all their thoughts. And all I had expected to see in Jaxon's mind was some gambling difficulties, a need for thrills and maybe something going on in his personal life.

But this was something else. Jaxon was a massive drug addict and I was amazed he wasn't brain dead with the amount of weed he smoked every day. But that's why he loved being a superhero because it took tons of weed to start affecting him. Then he used his poker winnings to buy drugs, and when they weren't enough he started to play the slots to get more.

Yet he only lost.

"What ya prob girl?" Jaxon said, clearly starting to get stoned.

I focused my calming and trusting superpowers on him, and he slowly started to look at me like a friend.

"You really should stop doing drugs," I said softly.

With my hand still on his shoulder I felt my minor command sink into his mind but his face didn't look impressed. He didn't want to stop doing drugs, and as much as I wanted to do properly therapy with him I really didn't like the colour of his aura.

It seemed like the more he smoked the red it got. And even the aura was starting to turn black around the edges.

Black meant death.

As much as I didn't want to even start to admit it, I was really starting to believe that Jaxon was going to die or end himself by tomorrow morning.

I almost couldn't blame him. He had no friends left in the superhero world, his family refused to talk to him and he was in extreme amounts of gambling debt. He had nothing to live for.

So I decided I needed to try a more direct path.

"I'm Matilda Plum, superhero in the Counselling and Therapy Sector," I said extending my hand.

Jaxon's eyes looked a little distant but he barely managed to shake my hand.

"Jaxon, superhero of… I donno. A sector,"

"People are worried about you Jaxon. They love you so why don't you tell me why you'll doing this destruction to yourself,"

Jaxon seemed to frown and smile and want to cry at the minor reminder of the damage he had caused. I focused my superpowers on making him want to feel like he wanted to change his ways.

"I just needed the thrills," he said. "Poker gets old quickly. I wanna smoke,"

He just started laughing as he smoked more and more. I knew I was going to have to do something a bit extreme but I didn't feel like I had another option.

I focused every ounce of influencing superpower to make him feel sick whenever he thought, looked or tasted any sort of drug, even caffeine.

Extreme I know, but I had to save him from himself.

He just started coughing and stamped out the cigarette. His aura only started to get darker and darker around the edges.

Then I implanted the suggestion of all the superheroes that were missing him, caring about him and wanted him to be okay deep into his mind.

He slowly smiled. "They really care about me?"

I wrapped an arm around his shoulder. "Of course. They're worried sick about you. They just want you to be okay and back being the amazing superhero you were,"

As Jaxon just stared out into space for a few moments, I wondered if the drugs had already taken affect too well. But he just sort of smiled and nodded.

"I want to see them too," Jaxon said. "What I need to do?"

I folded my arms and wondered about that myself. His difficulty was clearly caused by the drugs and gambling so if I could get him away completely from all of that for a while, so we could work on the other causes and anything else that might be causing his addiction. Then that would work.

He would have to be away from the internet (online poker), other people and everything else that could possibly make him relapse whilst he focused on me and his recovery. But it could work.

I actually might even know a great place we could stay for a while.

"You know," I said to Jaxon, "my boss Natalia, the Goddess of Counselling and Therapy, owns a wonderful villa on the coast of Italy we could stay for a month or two for your therapy. There's plenty of sun, sand and that sea view is just stunning,"

Jaxon really looked like he was going to hate it, and I honestly thought he was going to say no. But he started nodding, still frowning and gestured that he should get going.

"You sure you want to help your addiction?" I asked.

"Of course. I want to be back with my superhero friends and helping them out," he said.

But I just couldn't believe his heart was in it entirely, yet as a superhero, I had to try and help him as much as I could. Even if his heart wasn't completely in it.

\*\*\*

Now I had wanted to spend two months with Jaxon in that wonderful Italian villa so we could work on everything. And I mean everything! But that seriously hadn't happened and I was rather furious actually.

I walked into Octavia's large black office that was decorated in wonderful black tones, pictures of famous poker games and she was sitting at her massive black desk. I had to admit she looked stunning, sexy and just perfect in her little red dress that made her look so dangerous and alluring.

"Matilda darling, this is unexpected," Octavia said.

I just frowned at her. I always had a rule whenever I did these sorts of things with people like Jaxon. The rule was simple, they could leave at any time, because I was a therapist, I was not a prison guard.

But that always became risky when I was dealing with people as... "problematic" as Jaxon.

"Not in the slightest," I said. "His drug and gambling addiction is far worse than I ever imagined, and there is a reason why he doesn't want to stay,"

Octavia leant closer. "Why?"

"Because whenever people come to therapy, they have to be willing to change their behaviours because it is their behaviour that is causing the *problem*. Jaxon will never change or be willing to change,"

Octavia folded her arms. "You've done everything you can,"

My eyebrows rose. I was so used to being questioned in my

methods because I had a *psychology* degree I didn't know why I still reacted, but I had to admit it did hurt each and every time someone questioned me for no good reason.

I nodded.

Octavia stood there and then paced round her office for a few moments.

"Thank you," Octavia said with a killer smile. "Me, the other Gambling Superheroes and the God of Gambling himself thanks you,"

"What will happen to him?" I asked. "I've already dropped him off at a casino in London because he demanded it,"

Octavia kept smiling at me, and I couldn't help but feel like it was the sort of smile you give someone you wanted to do... and hard.

"I will report to the God of Gambling and he will most properly fire Jaxon and make him a normal person again," Octavia said before she disappeared.

I just wished I could do something else, this felt like such a failure, but I could honestly say I had tried everything with Jaxon.

But he just didn't want to change.

\*\*\*

Two weeks later I was walking along the wonderful cobblestone high street of Canterbury on a breathtakingly warm evening with the sounds of musicians playing, students drinking and talking when I got the news.

Jaxon Ellis had been found dead by a heroin overdose a few hours before, and as the air was filled with great hints of alcohol, rich Italian food and freshly baked garlic bread. I knew that there was nothing that I could have done.

You see as a therapist and superhero, it is my job to do my best with whoever I have to deal with. I love it. I get to help people improve their lives, stop their distress and help them in ways no one else can.

99% of the time, the job was amazing and it was more like play rather than work. Because it was so fun and I absolutely loved it.

But it was days like this when my hard "work" didn't pay off that honestly just felt shitty. And like everything I did just didn't matter and I was nothing more than a failure.

Yet I was never that. I always did my best, helped tons of people and most of all I allowed people to make their own choices. With all my superpowers I could easily bend people to my will, but I didn't. Because it was wrong and I really do believe in one particular therapy concept.

Everyone has to have a capacity to change.

And Jaxon Ellis did not.

He didn't want to help his addiction, so he was always going to end up like this sadly. I truly hated that fact.

But as I started to walk along the high street again, looking for someone else to help, I just knew there would be another time, another person, another opportunity to help someone.

And that time I would be able to. All because that person would have a capacity to change.

AUTHOR OF THE CITY OF ASSASSINS URBAN FANTASY SERIES

# CONNOR WHITELEY

## CRAZIEST WEDDING

A MATILDA PLUM FANTASY SHORT STORY

# CRAZIEST WEDDING

Weddings, love and marriages always have been rather strange to me. I've been in love tons of times but as most people know things don't always work out. I've also been married and had some weddings a few times, maybe five or six or even seven, but they all ended in similar ways. Divorce, murder and more death.

Now I understand if you think I'm some kind of cold psychopathic killer, but please relax, I am far, far from that.

You see my name is Matilda Plum, a superhero in the counselling, therapy and psychology sector. And I was most probably born in the 1890s or 1900s (it's hard to keep track when you're as old as I am) so there are plenty of chances to get married, fall in love and die.

And yes that order is very much correct, because back in the day you never married for love. And I should know my parents kept selling me and my siblings into marriages for ages, things kept happening to my husbands, but I heard most of my siblings learnt to fall in love with their husbands.

I'm more than happy that times have changed.

Anyway I'm standing next to a large apple tree on the grounds of the massive cathedral in Canterbury, England with its immense spires, large roman walls and gothic architecture that made it a perfect place for a wedding. Especially with the sun being perfectly warm and shining down upon a very happy couple.

I had no idea how the happy couple managed to get married in Canterbury Cathedral, besides the fact they must have had some killer connections, but they looked so perfect together.

The insanely hot man was wearing a tight waistcoat, trousers and silk shirt that made me feel like I was going to orgasm at any moment. He was that hot.

The equally stunning sexy wife looked so fit in her tight white wedding dress. And her hair... wow, her long brown hair was styled so perfectly that it only amplified the natural beauty of her face.

Both of them were so stunning that I would happily jump in there in a threesome if they requested it. And if I was an unethical superhero well... I do have an influencing superpower. Ha!

The air smelt so refreshing with hints of mint, pine and freshness that it really was the perfect day for a wedding. Especially with a very young man walking out wearing a very cute suit (this would turn into a foursome soon!) holding a very expensive camera. He was clearly the wedding photographer judging by how the couple were posing, but he was a tat young actually.

Then another person, a woman this time, came out and helped the photographer get ready. She was clearly a sister or something judging by the way the young man and woman were looking at each other. Half looking in love and respect, half looking in annoyance and frustration.

Then another woman of the same age came out of the cathedral and positioned the happy couple for the photo. She too was clearly a sister. Now this was slightly beyond me, three siblings all rather young and all helping the happy couple with their photographs.

Thankfully as a superhero psychologist all the myths, misconceptions and other rubbish I have to deal with normally, are now my superpowers so I can analyse them since they were talking to each other.

As I tapped into that superpower more and more I was completely shocked.

The woman was a serial killer who slaughtered her husbands in some... rather graphic fashions every year on the exact same date, granted there were sometimes a few weeks difference, but it was almost always about the same time.

Yet she couldn't remember how many people she had killed, what she had done with the bodies and if she enjoyed it or not.

I focused on the man and he was just as weird. He always killed his wives whenever the sex was lacking and he was... he was always going to kill them on the same exact day as the wife did. When these two actually got to killing each other that was going to be interesting.

But he also didn't know how many people he had killed, what he had done with the bodies and if he enjoyed it or not.

Neither one of them had a clue. It was flat out weird.

"Jack and Aiden!" I shouted.

The entire wedding party smiled and waved at me. I almost felt embarrassed then the world went blurry for a second and two men were standing next to me everything was okay.

Since the great thing about superheroes and Gods teleporting was we made sure everyone round us just thought the newly teleported person in was always there.

Aiden and Jack, my best friends and my employees as they were both superheroes in the same sector as me, folded their arms and just spat on the ground.

Normally people would imagine that was just flat out strange and disrespectful, but considering Aiden and Jack had been boyfriends for over a decade now, and both of them were even older than I was.

I had heard plenty of their stories from over the centuries where the religious leaders tortured them because they loved men, and it was unholy according to a two thousand year old text.

"Sorry guys. Wouldn't have bought you here if it wasn't urgent," I said.

They both weakly smiled at me.

"Tap into their minds and tell me what you see," I said.

They both shrugged, probably expecting to see a normal happily wedded couple. Then their faces turned to sadness, shock and horror as they focused back on me.

When they told me what they saw I just nodded because they saw the exact same as me.

"It's weird about them not knowing about if they liked it or not," Jack said.

I completely agreed. "New plan. Let's completely focus on the bride. All three of us focusing on her should help clarify the situation,"

They nodded and we all focused our superpowers on the bride.

Now there were two other superheroes helping me, her mind was a lot easier to understand and there were so many levels here that it was fascinating to see.

Then I figured it out.

I directed the images I saw back to Aiden and Jack as I finished with them. It seemed there were never any real killings, murders or anything illegal, it was all make believe.

And the more and more I unpeeled the layers of this woman, the more passion I realised she felt towards the groom. Because he was always the same husband, she had married him when she was eighteen, they kept having sex then a year later they started arguing. A LOT.

So in one of their fights they both shouted about would the other one be sad if they died. Both said they would be heartbroken and completely lost without each other, because they truly, truly did love each other.

In the crazy end of this massive fight both of them faked their own deaths, move to another city and started the romance all over again.

They had done this eight times now.

And the three very, very young adults showing the photos were from their first marriage, but I was completely shocked at how close they all were.

The children of course found it was a little weird their parents kept doing this, but it only seemed to make the family stronger.

Me, Jack and Aiden pulled out of the wife and immediately searched the husband's mind. He only confirmed everything but my god was he horny.

I had never been inside such a horny man. All he wanted to do was rip off his wife's wedding dress and start the romance all over again until they died.

It was so strange!

After the three of us pulled out again, we all slowly started to walk away, down a little block-paved street towards the high street. We all sort of just walked in silence for a little while, just letting the craziness of it all sink in.

Then Jack kissed Aiden on the cheek. "I would want to make us work no matter what,"

Aiden really smiled at his boyfriend and kissed him.

"I do to. I just hope we never go to that extreme," he said.

The two lovebirds wrapped their arms round each other's waist as we walked and I realised they were completely right.

Sure the married couple definitely had the craziest wedding I had ever come across, but it wasn't hurting anyone. Meaning it didn't fall under our job to interfere and help with, and I was fine with that.

In fact I was glad about it. I was really glad that those two (seriously hot) people had found a way to make their lives, love and romance work in a way that suited them.

I felt Aiden's and Jack's horniness radiate off them, and I just nodded to them.

They teleported away and I was pretty sure they were going to make their bed very, very messy this afternoon. And after being inside the groom's mind, I seriously understood that.

So I was definitely going to call a *special friend* of mine too, because isn't it only polite to make adult fun after attending a wedding?

I think so. And I sure as hell wasn't going to waste this excuse!

AUTHOR OF THE CITY OF ASSASSINS URBAN FANTASY SERIES

# CONNOR WHITELEY

# STRUGGLES AMONGST LOST

A MATILDA PLUM FANTASY SHORT STORY

# STRUGGLES AMONGST LOST

After living for so, so long I find it extremely hard to remember when I was actually born, before I remember running messages across the frontlines on my motorbike during the Great War so it was definitely before then. Then I was alive in world war two and I am still now.

So needless to say I know lost. I have no family still alive, no friends from my childhood and during those two wars alone I had lost more people than I ever thought possible.

Sure it was damn right impossible to deal with some deaths. Like the death of my family when the Nazis bombed our family home, deaths like the murder of my first ever proper boyfriend and girlfriend, and the list just goes on and on and on.

Death is just a part of life.

And of course that might sound extremely harsh, but after you've lived for over a century or more you learn ways to help yourself through the inevitably harsh times when someone you loved dies.

You see I can live forever (at least biologically speaking) because my name is Matilda Plum, a superhero in the counselling, therapy and psychology sector. Meaning it is my job (and utter passion) to help people solve their difficulties, improve their lives and maintain their mental health.

And death comes in a lot in my psychology practice in Canterbury, England. Most of the time when it comes to death, I tend to see people who are in deep down depression because of someone they love died.

But not always.

I sometimes have the amazingly fun job of travelling up to some of the UK's most secure prisons and talking to psychopaths, serial killers and other foul people thanks to my superhero friends in the prison, justice and policing sector.

As I sat in my favourite hard wooden chair in my therapist room with its large white walls with tasteful colour art hanging on them (none of that modern art crap was allowed), and my wide range of chairs for people to enjoy, I was starting to look forward to my next appointment.

The really interesting thing about this particular appointment was she had specifically requested the smell of lavender, grapefruit and passionfruit to be in the office for when she came in.

Now I became a superhero funny enough on the day Hitler invaded Poland so I have been helping people with their mental health for over 80 years (bloody hell!) and I have never had a request like that.

"Miss Plum?" someone said, knocking on the door.

As much as I wanted to wait the extra five minutes until the woman's appointment actually began, so I could enjoy the amazing smell and the taste of passion fruit cheesecake it left on my tongue, I decided that I better help her as soon as possible.

I went to the door and welcomed in the client, explained how the therapy would work and the other legal things I needed to cover. But this woman seemed to already know it all.

It's not necessarily that's strange, but if this woman had been in therapy before then it was perfectly natural for her to know this. But my spidey sense was telling me it was something else.

The woman was rather attractive in a way and I really liked her long blond hair, well-fitting (and suggestive) purple dress and her purple high-heels. She looked great but she didn't look like she was here for a therapy session.

As I watched her tit-ass-about trying to choose a seat (I mean I have a wide range of different chairs to choose from but it isn't an exam. Just choose one!), I kept seeing her flick back at me. Almost like she wanted to know exactly where I was the entire time.

"Is everything okay?" I asked.

She smiled as she pulled over a large blue beanbag and sat on it. I did the same out of politeness more than anything else.

Once we were both sitting down and comfortable I was about to tap into my analysis superpower when I felt her trying to do the same to me.

This woman was a superhero or something.

But then why would this woman be trying to analyse me? This wasn't normal, right or fair in the slightest.

"Enough," I said calmly into her mind.

She frowned.

"Who are you?" I asked.

"Eris Junior," she said.

My eyes widened. That meant she was the daughter of the Greek God of Mischief and chaos. What the hell was she doing here?

I felt myself sink into the beanbag and my hands and feet became trapped inside. I couldn't move.

"What do you know about the Rogue God?" she asked.

I just shook my head. Me and my friends had been dealing with a Rogue God that was commanding people to hurt themselves and completely abusing the powers given to us, but I still had no idea what was going on.

My boss, Natalia was meant to be investigating since she was a Goddess herself, but I hadn't heard anything for ages. So it was slightly beyond strange that Eris Junior was asking.

"Why you want to know?" I asked.

Eris Junior grinned at me. I sank further into the beanbag.

"Stop that," I said firmly.

She kept smiling. I kept sinking. I tried to fight it.

I tapped into her mind. I commanded her to stop. She didn't listen.

I focused more and more. She still didn't listen. I sank faster and faster.

"Natalia!" I shouted.

Eris's eyes widened. She kept grinning. My boss didn't turn up.

That never happened. Normally whenever I shouted her name she came running to help me.

She wasn't here.

"I am a superhero of Mischief and chaos and confusion," Eris Junior said. "Your friends think they are with you, having dinner and talking with them. They don't know you are with me,"

My eyes widened. That was flat out impossible, I didn't want to know why Eris Junior had created a body double of me, but it was clearly real and I was in danger.

"Why?" I asked.

Eris stood up and wrapped her hands round my throat.

"I want to know about the Rogue God,"

I could only smile as she was touching me, my influencing and analysis superpowers worked in a lot of very fun ways. I could analyse someone if they were speaking or touching or merely looking at me. I was that good, and Eris Junior was that stupid.

Her mind was interesting and rather like a playground. But I knew her mind was more akin to a rose garden, something beautiful with deadly spikes, rather than a playground to read and study and enjoy.

Whoever had helped her out with all this mind work had clearly wanted me to read her mind probably and wanted me to mentally injure myself in the process.

I pulled straight out of her mind.

Yet that mindscaping and forcing her mind to work in such specific ways so that it would be dangerous for me took some extreme skill. Again, no superhero could do that sort of work, only a god or goddess could.

"Do you know who the Rogue God is?" Eris Junior asked. "I do,"

I seriously doubted that for some reason, after all she was a superhero of mischief.

"Do you want me to tell you?" she asked.

She whipped out a knife. Pressing it against my nose.

"I could tell you but then I'll have to kill you,"

She was bat crap crazy this woman!

Then I realised something very important about this entire thing.

"Wait, you have a body double of me," I said.

She took her hands off my throat, came in front of me and nodded.

"And that would require a mental connection between me and the body double, correct?"

She frowned. I was right.

"You stupid idiot," I said. "You might be clever in your mischief but the mind and human behaviour is my domain,"

I closed my eyes and really focused on myself. I felt my superpowers coursing through my mind and I found it. I found a very large shadowy ball in my mind that was never meant to be there.

I had no doubt that shadowy ball was connected to the body double with my friends.

"Fuck you bitches!" I shouted into the shadowy ball. Hoping my body double would say that to my friends.

And the one thing I never did to my friends was insult them.

Eris Junior jumped me.

My hands and feet were still sunk in the bean bag. They couldn't move. Eris threw me to the ground.

My wrists and ankles snapped.

I screamed in agony.

Crippling pain filled me.

Eris Junior smashed her fists into me.

Again.

And again.

My nose broke.

Golden fire shot into Eris Junior.

Throwing her against the wall.

A few moments later a stunningly sexy woman with a long golden dress, golden glowing hair and the most beautiful face I have ever seen stepped over me. Natalia, Goddess of counselling, therapy and psychology blasted Eris Junior with another fireball.

My pain grew in intensity.

I collapsed into unconsciousness.

\*\*\*

A few hours later I woke up on my wonderfully soft and cool sofa in my therapist room staring up at my bright white ceiling. As much as I wanted to move I knew I couldn't just yet, I still felt a little weak after the attack.

Thankfully my wrists and ankles were perfectly healed, fixed and felt as good as new. Believe me, I was more than pleased about that and I just knew that Natalia was behind it.

The air smelt amazing of hints of mint, pine and other refreshing scents that I couldn't quite identify, I immediately knew why Eris Junior had requested the strange scents of lavender, grapefruit and passionfruit earlier. Because according to superhero folklore they increased the powers of mischief superheroes.

I doubted it, but maybe I should reconsider that opinion.

"You okay?" I heard a man say.

I slowly forced myself up and I sat carefully on my sofa, and truly smiled as I saw my best friends were all around me. Natalia was still glowing and beautiful as always, then my fellow superheroes and employees Jack and Aiden were there too.

It was so, so good to see them.

"What happened?" I asked weakly.

Natalia smiled. "You swore at us. We knew something was wrong so I teleported here and found Eris,"

I only frowned at her name. "I think she's working with the Rogue God,"

Natalia nodded. "She has been imprisoned and interrogated for her crimes. She will never see the light of day again but I believe I am one step closer to finding out who is behind this,"

"Thank God... Goddess," I said.

We laughed and Natalia kissed me on the head (I absolutely loved her power, chemistry and electricity flow between us) then she disappeared.

Me, Jack and Aiden sat in silence as I just hated to imagine that this Rogue God now had superheroes being corrupted and falling to his side. I hated that idea.

Because Eris Junior had really proved a point in all honesty, she had clearly been struggling with herself, and that's why she had been so easy for a God to bend her to his will, since Eris Junior was really only a puppet.

I didn't know exactly whatever mindscaping or suggestions this Rogue God added to her, but I had a very good sense he had a few extra commands. Believe me no superhero would have attacked another without being commanded to.

It just wasn't how the world worked.

So I actually had little doubt that Eris Junior had died in some fashion, been replaced with an alternative one and that was the struggle we were all facing.

How the hell did a superhero fall to the evil of the Rogue God?

As much as I wanted to find out, that was certainly tomorrow's problem, so I simply got up and grabbed my two best friends.

"Fancy a real dinner with me?" I asked.

Jack smiled. "You gonna swear at us again?"

I just playfully hit them both as we teleported away. "You know I don't swear you little shits,"

AUTHOR OF THE CITY OF ASSASSINS URBAN FANTASY SERIES

# CONNOR WHITELEY

## WOMAN IN PRIDEFUL HEAT

A MATILDA PLUM FANTASY SHORT STORY

# WOMAN IN PRIDEFUL HEAT

I had always flat out loved the annual Pride Festival in Canterbury England. I loved the happiness, colours and just how amazing everyone at the Pride event was. They were always so kind, generous and very protective of everyone else at the event, regardless of whether you were straight or gay or somewhere in-between.

But I still made sure I went every year, mainly because I always wanted to show my unwavering support for these people, and I was technically bisexual myself, but most importantly because I did it as part of my job.

You see my name is Matilda Plum, a superhero in the counselling, therapy and psychology sector. So these pride events are perfect for me since it is my job to travel around, help people solve their problems and protect their mental health.

Yet it is a very sad truth that pride events are almost like breeding grounds for my sort of help, but there are always people here who really want to experience their gay side but they feel extremely guilty because of their homophobic family. Other people simply need a little push in the right direction to feel at home here. And other people still are just conflicted about being so-called "normal" (whatever the fuck that means) and being who they really are.

As I started to walk down the wonderfully warm cobblestone high street with little shops lining the streets with their pride flags and special discounts because of the event.

I had already helped two young men who were on the verge of suicide, but I helped them to realise they weren't demonically possessed and that they were normal people that deserved happiness.

The sound of the music echoed all around canterbury as the event and parade and parties continued into the late afternoon. The amazing smell of cooking sausages, burgers and French fries filled the local parks and high street as everyone was looking forward to tonight's entertainment.

At these events I always made sure I bought the sexual essentials in case someone ever took an interest in me, and I was taught at a very early age (before I became a superhero actually) that if a good looking person wants to have sex with you. It was fairly rude to say no.

I stuck to the outside of the massive crowd of people as we all walked down the high street towards the massive park where the concerts, food and other activities were happening.

And then I noticed something.

Normally whenever someone was in trouble my superpowers would sort of pull me in that direction and that's what they were doing now. They were telling me to go away from the crowd and start walking back up the high street.

That alone was weird enough since everyone (and I really do mean everyone) was heading down the high street.

As I always refused to argue with my superpowers I started walking back up the high street, and saw my two employees and fellow superheroes in the same sector as me, Jack and Aiden.

I gestured them to walk with me and they did.

To be honest I was a bit surprised they looked as *straight* as they did. Both Jack and Aiden were wearing tight black jeans, blue shirts and blue trainers. But besides from that the two boyfriends only had a gay flag painted on their cheeks, compared to other people here today they really weren't making much of an effort.

At least they looked a bit more comfortable than me, I was really starting to regret wearing a white blouse, black trousers and high heels. It wasn't completely my fault as I did need to work in our mental health practice this morning to help some people. But these heels were killing me!

"Sense what we are?" Jack asked me.

I nodded. It must have been major if all three of us were sensing it.

Then further up the high street I noticed that a woman was glowing slightly. I quickly realised she had a black aura around herself.

"Black aura," I said.

Me and Jack and Aiden quickly walked towards her, because a black aura only meant one thing. Death.

When we got to the woman she was rocking and bumping and crashing through the crowd towards us. But she wasn't making any sounds.

As superhero psychologists the three of us would be able to analyse her if she said anything. But she was clearly too drunk or high or something to do anything.

As she stumbled towards us, I had to admit she was beautiful. She clearly wasn't wearing a bra that I seriously didn't mind, her white shirt was soaked through and her jeans had clearly seen better days.

But why was she sweating?

The three of us quickly went over to her as she exited the crowd and fell on the ground.

Jack and Aiden grabbed her and pulled over and sat her down outside a nearby closed shop. The woman was sweating, crying and she was a mess.

But she was making a sound.

I concentrated all my strength on my analysing superpower and focused on what on was happening. I managed to get into her mind. And wow this woman was horny.

I had never been inside such a horny mind. She wanted to do everyone at the event, woman, man, transgender she wanted it all.

It was so hard to concentrate as her mind was getting more and more horny every second. It was like being drugged every second.

Maybe she was?

"What did you take?" I asked.

The woman smiled as her eyes went glassy.

Her aura went pitch black.

"We're losing her!" Aiden shouted.

Jack started to call the paramedics. Thankfully there were always paramedics nearby at these events.

I knelt down next to Aiden.

"What you got?" Aiden asked.

I shrugged. Focusing all of my superpowers on her. I really burrowed into her mind.

She was angry deep down. She had just split up from her boyfriend in London and she wanted to restart life. So she came down here and took some drugs.

They were drugs that her boyfriend had given her to help become more free. The bastard had drugged his own ex!

That was disgraceful.

"I need to see her ex. I'll be quick," I said.

The woman collapsed to the floor.

Aiden started CPR.

I had to hurry.

\*\*\*

I was going to make this bastard pay for hurting his ex-girlfriend. I quickly teleported to the address I had pulled out of the woman's mind and this was not what I was expecting.

Knowing how foul the boyfriend was from the woman's mind, I had been expecting a dirty apartment filled with weed smoke, drugs and just a disgusting apartment.

But that was far from the case as I appeared in a large perfectly clean apartment with a very white modern kitchen, the finest furniture and a very hot man staring at me.

Thankfully because of how my teleporting works the man would just assume I have always been in the apartment for at least a minute before I actually was. But wow, this man was hot in his fine Italian silk suit, gold watch and just… wow!

"What?" he asked.

I just closed my eyes and started humming a very seductive tune and when I opened my eyes a second later. He was completely unconscious and I focused on what his mind had to tell me.

It wasn't hard to find the name of the drug he had given her, but he seriously loved her, he cared about her and it turned out she wasn't as bad in bed as the woman believed.

The benefits of being in two minds.

"Matilda!" Aiden shouted into my mind.

I had to return.

The woman was dying.

I had to save her.

\*\*\*

I quickly jumped back to the high street and the paramedics just nodded at me like I had always been there. I quickly told them the name of the drug and they looked a lot happier.

The paramedics pulled out something from their medical bags, injected her with it and the woman's black aura disappeared.

Me and Aiden and Jack all knew that the woman would be fine now that the black aura was gone, so the three of us gently used our superpowers to suggest the paramedics to leave. At least they would be free to help other people now.

The paramedics smiled, told the woman to go to hospital if she felt worse and they left.

The entire high street was a lot emptier now the vast majority of people had moved onto the park, and me and the love boyfriends looked at the woman as she slowly become more and more aware of her surroundings.

"My head's killing me," she said.

I laughed. "Yea. I'm guessing you overdosed on those pills your boyfriend gave you,"

I could sense her discomfort at me talking about him.

"He does love you. He really loves you," I said. "and you're actually a lot better in bed than you think according to him,"

A massive smile lit the woman's face. "Really?"

"Of course. He loved you so much that he was heartbroken about the idea of you dying. He wants to be with you forever," I said.

The woman slowly got up and her eyebrows rose.

"How do you know?" she asked.

Me and Aiden and Jack all looked at each other and smiled.

"We're psychologists," we all said.

The woman quickly nodded like we were amazing all-known people because of our jobs then she quickly ran away in case we analysed her anymore.

Some of the myths people believe about us is just amazing.

I wrapped my arms around Jack's and Aiden's, and we all started to walk back down the high street, because after saving a woman's life I definitely needed some Pride fun.

Meaning dancing, eating and most importantly being around people that loved you.

And that really did sound like the perfect evening to me.

AUTHOR OF THE CITY OF ASSASSINS URBAN FANTASY SERIES

# CONNOR WHITELEY

# A MAGIC PROBLEM

A MATILDA PLUM FANTASY SHORT STORY

# A MAGIC PROBLEM

Human beings can think about some very, very weird things, but they can think about very normal things too. Some people think about sex a LOT (I like those people), other people think about their families, loved ones and jobs, then there are other people who think about weird things.

I don't really know what my weirdest find ever was, but I think it would have to be a young woman I came across a few years ago who wanted herself and her boyfriend to lose their virginity to each other, and wow. She had clearly watched way too much fantastical porn.

Thankfully I simply slipped in a few helpful tips for her and she... she certainly had a good night.

Oh yea, I should probably clarify. My name is Matilda Plum a superhero in the counselling, therapy and psychology sector. So quite often I have to slip into the minds of people helping them solve their problems, their psychological distress and improve their lives.

And I love it!

Today I was out with one of my best friends, a fellow superhero in the same sector (and my employee) Aiden as we went round a massive shopping centre walking on the top marble floor near some jewellery shops.

The shopping centre was easily the size of twenty football pitches with very posh shops, plenty of food courts and about every single shop a person could ask for.

The sound of people muttering, talking and complaining about how many people were here today echoed around the entire shopping centre. It was almost like all the sound rolled into one constant drone of sounds without even my superpower abilities able to pick out individual voices.

But I did enjoy the amazing smell of crispy fried chicken, succulent pork chops and spicy cheesy fries that flowed up from the food court below us. I was definitely going to have to steer Aiden in that direction later on, with the amazing taste of a fried chicken dinner forming on my very hungry tongue.

Granted it might have been extremely busy in here today but it wasn't too hot not cold. Thankfully the shopping centre had some killer air-conditioning that managed to help everyone stay cool, happy and kept them shopping.

Very clever.

Me and Aiden were walking past a very expensive jewellery store with ten thousand pound necklaces, rings and bracelets firmly displayed on the outside enticing us to go inside.

Aiden looked like he was seriously considering something for himself or his boyfriend Jack. I was a little more cautious, because whilst both of us could easily afford to buy the entire shopping centre without any hint of bankruptcy. I just wasn't sure if the money was worth it.

Aiden went over to the store and focused on a very expensive rose gold bracelet with diamonds embedded into the metal. I have to admit it did look stunning, but seriously?

I was about to suggest we should move on in case we found someone who did need our help, but then I realised my spidey sense was going off.

I couldn't help but think someone in the store was in trouble, and judging by the massive smile on Aiden's face, he had sensed it too. Probably before me.

Then I noticed he wasn't actually looking at the bracelet he was looking past the window and into the store.

"Fine smartass," I said quietly to Aiden. "Pretend to be buying me the bracelet,"

Aiden laughed. "Pretend? I was gonna buy it for Jack,"

I almost threw up my arms up in the air. "Fine, buy it for me in the store. Then give it to Jack,

Aiden kissed me on the cheek. I quickly noted down the item number or code was probably a more accurate way of putting it.

Me and Aiden went into the large oval jewellery store with a massive ring of glass cabinets lining the store and then there was another ring of counters in the middle. Everything looked so amazing, beautiful and stunning.

And I realised that Aiden in his black business suit, black shoes and perfectly styled hair was a lot more suited to this store than I was, in my far more casual jeans, a white blouse and dyed black hair.

There was a very fit six foot six man in a tight black waistcoat, trousers and smooth-shaven face that smiled at us, and me and Aiden almost raced over to see him.

He was the hottest looking man I had seen for ages and he was so young, probably 25, and wow… just wow he was hot.

"Hello I would like to buy item EQ24 for my lady please," Aiden said.

The man almost looked disappointed at Aiden, probably for acting straight. I just smiled.

"Of course Sir," the man said and gestured Aiden to go with him to get the item back out of the front display windows.

Whilst they were gone I really focused on the surroundings of the store, I had been so captured so that hot sexy man that I hadn't had a chance to focus on the other customers.

There weren't too many which made sense considering the price of the store, but there were three other male staff members (that were equally hot as our server), a rich young couple with the husband holding a briefcase and a very non-rich couple.

I liked the non-rich couple because you could sort of tell that they only in here pretending to be rich, but they were so polite, kind and funny that I really liked that. And their server seemed to be fine.

That's why my spidey sense kicked into action and I focused on the man serving the non-rich couple. He was wearing the same waistcoat and trousers as our hot man, but he was slightly older (maybe 30) and there was just something wrong about him.

He still had beautiful eyes, and…

Come to think of it, I couldn't deny that everyone in this store was a little too attractive. Yea, it's normal for businesses to hire attractive staff members to help sales, but it is not normal for them to be attractive in the exact same ways.

Me and Aiden were talking years ago about our past boyfriends and there was never a repeat of what we found attractive about them. For example, my first ever boyfriend I liked because of his squarish face and white teeth. My next boyfriend I liked because of his funny attitudes and his smile. My last boyfriend (and yes of course there were men and women in-between) I found attractive because of his… wayward parts.

But everyone in this entire store was attractive because of their bodies, handsome faces and politeness. That wasn't natural.

So as Aiden came over to me looking worried, I knew he had figured out the same, and I tapped into my analysis superpower (the perks of being a superhero psychologist).

I found nothing.

It was almost like none of these people had minds at all. They didn't have any wants, memories or desires. It was so strange.

My spidey sense activated again and I focused on the rich couple. I analysed them and found they wanted to kill the non-rich couple for daring to insult their richness just because they were too stupid and poor to buy the things they could.

Aiden came close to me. "I think we need a bit of help,"

I nodded.

"Natalia come out of time please!" I shouted.

A moment later the entire store went icy cold and blurry as Natalia, Goddess of counselling, therapy and psychology appeared next to me.

Everyone was completely frozen in-between the moments in time except me, Natalia and Aiden.

And even though I had worked with Natalia tons of times now, I still couldn't get over how stunningly beautiful she was with her long golden hair, amazingly fit body and her divine sexual power that radiated off her (or maybe that's just a fantasy of mine!).

Then I noticed how creepy, silent and awful being frozen in time was. It was so unnatural because there was no sound whatsoever despite the background noise being rather deafening only moments ago.

Natalia frowned at the three staff members. "Have you analysed them?"

Both and Aiden nodded.

Natalia stared at us and her eyes glowed bright gold. I felt her burrowed into the deepest darkest depths of my soul and it felt strange.

Then Natalia did the same to Aiden but more intensely.

"These people have come into contact with dark magic," Natalia said.

I gasped. I knew superheroes, Gods and Goddesses were real but I didn't know about magic.

I focused on the jewels and realised that all of them were just a bit too enticing.

"They must have used them on the jewels," I said.

Natalia nodded. "These people were fools. Using magic for self-fish reasons never ends well and now this people have probably infected others with the dark magic,"

Aiden shook his head and held his hand above the jewellery.

"I can sense the magic in the jewels. You think everyone who has ever bought them is in danger of becoming infected?" Aiden asked.

Natalia nodded.

I hated to think about all the thousands of people who could be infected with dark magic, and I hated even more to imagine how many might die from it.

Natalia extended her fingers towards all three of the staff members and the jewels in the store. She zapped them with her own superpowers.

"They're safe… but be ready to see what they actually look like," Natalia said with an evil grin.

Me and Aiden nodded.

"I'll get the store's records and work with other Gods and superheroes in the other sectors to hunt down these jewels and destroy the dark magic,"

"Thank you," me and Aiden said.

Natalia disappeared and the sound slammed back into me.

And I was shocked at what I saw.

I was completely surprised to see the three staff members turn into elderly men with bald patches all over their heads, their suits were nothing more than rags and the jewels were clearly fake.

I just looked the hot man who served us.

"Shit," he said.

The sound of the non-rich couple laughing their heads off made me smile as at least someone was enjoying themselves. But I sensed the rage coming from the rich-couple, there was such hatred in their eyes that I had to act.

I focused on the woman of the rich couple. Aiden focused on

the man. We burrowed into their minds using our influencing superpowers and I was going to make them regret thinking about them.

It was rather simple actually. I simply made them forget about wanting to kill the non-rich couple.

And I implanted a few suggestions to make sure this would never happen again.

I made sure whenever the woman thought about killing she would start crying like a baby. Whenever the woman wanted to judge someone because of their class or amount of money, she would slap herself across the face as hard as she could. And whenever she couldn't help herself to buying something nice, she would be compelled to buy the same item again and give it to someone less fortunate.

I pulled out of her mind and just started laughing. Aiden pulled out a few moments later and he fell onto the floor laughing.

The husband took his briefcase and swung it as hard as he could into his balls. He hissed and fell to the ground in agony.

The wife slapped herself across the face leaving a very bright red mark.

"I think our work is done," I said.

Aiden nodded. "Work? Don't you mean play?"

I just laughed at that.

Because he was absolutely right.

\*\*\*

After helping two depressed people at the shopping centre realise what was causing their depression and what to do about it, me and Aiden came back to my practice, told Jack about our adventure and now we were all sitting in my office.

I really did love the white bright walls, my very modern desk and how sweet smelling it all smelt, it was a very relaxing smell, and with no clients being in the practice it was perfectly silent.

It turned out Jack had held down the fort very well whilst we were out and he had helped a lot of people, which was just flat out brilliant news. I knew he was a great superhero.

A moment later everything went blurry for a moment and Natalia appeared. But she didn't look like her normal beautiful self, in fact she looked rather drained.

I offered her a seat and surprisingly enough she denied it.

"I came to inform you about our hunt," Natalia said.

"Did you find everything?" Jack asked.

Natalia frowned. "Negative. Or yes in a way. We found all two thousand jewels that contained the dark magic and stripped the magic out of the jewels, the owners and the homes they were in,"

I leant forward. "I sense there's a but,"

"I got my friend the God of Security, Magical Defences and Chastity, don't ask, to look at the case. And he found something very disturbing,"

As much as I wanted to know what the hell chastity had to do with magic and security, I felt like Natalia was a lot more disturbed than she was letting on.

"It seems like the three elderly men didn't just find the dark magic one day, and the dark magic corrupted them and their business. Someone infected them with the dark magic first,"

Me, Jack and Aiden just gasped. That was something beyond evil, it was one thing to become corrupted by dark magic. But for someone to willingly infect others, that was monstrous.

But I think I understood where she was going with this, there had been an incident only a few weeks ago about a rogue god infecting the mind of someone with mental commands that would kill them over time. That was a horrific thing to do.

And I had a terrible sense that this was another incident.

"The rogue god or goddess?" I asked.

Natalia slowly nodded.

Jack and Aiden looked furious and I didn't blame them. It was disgusting that a god would do such a terrible thing.

"I will keep investigating but I will get Gods and Goddesses that I trust involved because clearly this rogue is getting more and more dangerous,"

I nodded my thanks and Natalia disappeared.

All three of us just sort of sat in silence for a moment as the tension and reality of the situation sunk in. But there was really nothing more the three of us could do for a while, we were superhero psychologists, not detectives.

So finding this rogue god would certainly be a waiting game and tomorrow's problem.

And there was something a lot more important to do first.

I took Jack's and Aiden's hands and smiled.

"You know Jack, Aiden was going to buy you a very nice bracelet today, and because I helped him stop some dark magic from destroying lives. I think he should buy me one too," I said.

We all laughed at that and teleported off to another shopping centre to treat ourselves to some very nice jewellery.

Because we have the money, friendship and positive thoughts, and if you can't make use of them, then what's the point?

AUTHOR OF THE CITY OF ASSASSINS URBAN FANTASY SERIES

# CONNOR WHITELEY

# CONFLICTING SUPERHERO SUGGESTIONS

A MATILDA PLUM FANTASY SHORT STORY

# CONFLICTING SUPERHERO SUGGESTIONS

On the whole I think it is fairly safe to say that humans are very suggestible people. From the media to politics to the choices of clothes we choose to wear, everything is designed to influence and suggest choices to us.

Now this isn't always a bad thing, suggestions about healthy food, better lifestyles and ways to improve our mental health are never bad things. And that is where I come in.

My name is Matilda Plum, a superhero in the counselling, therapy and psychology sector, and my job is very enjoyable and I really do love it. I get to go round helping people, improving lives and making sure their mental health is okay.

Suggestions can be a large part of my work (Ha. It seems cruel to call what I do work. I love it so much.) because a very large part of therapy is about suggesting and helping people to decrease their distress and improve their lives.

But this isn't exactly how my perfectly planned Wednesday afternoon was going to turn out.

You see I was in my "therapist room" (I only call it that because apparently I cannot have two offices. Stupid rules) which was a wonderfully large room with white walls, colourful real art (not that modern art crap) and a wide range of comfortable chairs scattered about. Since I find that different people prefer different chairs, and so do I depending on the person or client I'm helping.

If I'm helping a child, they tend to love beanbag chairs which I have in the corner. Some adults love my surprisingly comfortable wooden chairs. And some teenagers... well teenagers are a very mixed bag.

So my plan for the afternoon was to have a two hour session with a brand new client who wouldn't tell me what difficulties he was having over the phone, so I booked a two hour session as I felt there would be a lot more to work through in the first session than I thought.

Then I planned to spend the rest of the afternoon doing some paperwork before I went out with some superhero friends from different sectors.

But the closer it got to my two hour appointment the more and more my awareness superpower, or spidey sense as others called it, was telling me something was very, very wrong.

I decided to check my therapist room, but everything was as it should be and the last hints of lavender, jasmine and soothing orange was going. It was one of my favourite smells but new clients had rather firmly told me they didn't always like it. But other clients loved it. That was just weird sometimes.

I also went over to my glass door in case my two other counselling superhero employees were in trouble. But nope. I could clearly hear Jack and Aiden in their rooms helping their own clients, they were okay.

Nothing seemed to be wrong.

I was just about to go over to my desk when there was a very loud knock at the door. I have never understood why people feel the need to slam and knock and bash on my door, but I suppose it's a small problem in the grand scheme of things.

When I opened the door and let in my two hour appointment, I couldn't help but focus on him. He wasn't a very attractive man per se but I just felt the need to focus on him. Normally I only studied a man or woman like this if they were hot but this man was not.

I carefully let him in, choose a seat and he laughed to himself and muttered something about this being a likely test. It wasn't. But still I just focused on him in his black jeans, long blue shirt and brown shoes. He clearly worked somewhere where he had to look professional, but I still didn't know why I had to keep looking at him.

We both introduced ourselves as he sat on a very comfortable but hard wooden chair. I did the same and was surprised he was called Richard Baker, he looked more like a Donald to me, but that didn't matter.

Since he had spoken to me I tapped into my analysis

superpowers (the benefits of being a superhero psychologist) and got to see he was very disturbed about night time.

It seems when it got dark he would cry himself to sleep, whenever he thought about cooking a chicken dinner he would hit himself in the balls and he would just start confessing his love for his wife whenever someone mentioned love.

Now I was curious.

Because to me these all sounded like suggestions implanted in his mind by a superhero. You see when us superheroes depending on the sector, come into contact with a disgusting person who does horrific things we like to... make sure we use our superpowers for good. Making sure the idiots we deal with never do it again.

"Tell me Mr Baker, why do you think you keep hitting yourself and crying?" I asked.

For a few moments he looked terrified that I actually knew what was going on, then he smiled and just thought I knew because I was a psychologist.

It was because I was a superhero one, but that wasn't too important now.

Yet he just shrugged.

"I dunno know. Just kept doing it ever since I found a website,"

It would be quicker for me to search his mind but I wanted to hear him tell me.

"What website?"

He looked around. "Is everything I say confidential?"

I nodded. I had already explained that to him in our introductions but I could sense how embarrassed, frustrated and just annoyed he was acting like this. If he was a normal client I would gently help him to realise it was okay to be acting like this as I got him to understand there were better ways to behave and cope with life.

But he was far from a normal client. He was a possibly foul person, well he had to be for a superhero to implant these suggestions into his mind.

"What website did you look at?" I asked.

Richard looked at the floor. "A sexist one. A Wife beater one. A really bad one,"

I leant closer. I shouldn't have but again he wasn't a normal client, especially as me and my superhero friends had had to deal with a similar website a few weeks earlier.

We had targeted the website because of all the sexist pigs who were beating their wives and killing innocent women.

There was a chance this was one of those beaters.

"I only looked for a few minutes. I responded to some comments, I…"

"You were supporting their beatings," I said, impressed there wasn't a hint of judgement in my voice.

Richard nodded. "I thought they were joking. I thought the picture of dead women were… jokes,"

It took all my superhero effort not to judge him, hit him or deal with him.

He punched himself in the balls.

And when I tapped into his mind, I was surprised to see he hadn't wanted to hurt me, which we all agreed was the standard command we would give those horrible men. So why was this man punching himself in the balls if he didn't want to hurt me, a woman?

I looked up. "Natalia! James! Love birds!"

A second later everything turned blurry for and then everything fell silent and Richard was frozen like a statue as Natalia, the Goddess of Counselling, Therapy and Psychology slipped us in-between moments of time.

As a woman who loved both women and men, seeing Natalia was always a special treat with her amazing golden dress, amazingly fit body and the sheer sexual power that radiated off her. She was stunning, but as she was a Goddess (no wonder) and my boss I was hardly even going to do anything.

Moments later James, Jack and Aiden, all superheroes in my sector teleported in all wearing smart suits, black shoes and golden watches, and as both Jack and Aiden looked worried I knew they must be at a critical moment in counselling their own clients.

Yet as they were boyfriends I quickly felt their worry run away.

"Why did you call us Matty dear?" Natalia asked.

I just pointed to Richard. "He was one of the targets on our hit list for the sexist website,"

James laughed. "Then he deserved what he got,"

I wanted to agree with him but I still wasn't so sure he was a guilty person.

"I don't think he was sexist and the idiot pigs like the rest of the targets," I said.

Natalia folded her arms. And when a Goddess folded her arms like that, I really wanted to run.

"What you want us to do?" Aiden asked.

"Does anyone recognise him from their list?" I asked.

Each of my friends looked at Richard intensely, and I was really glad he was frozen in time otherwise he might have died from a heart attack. Having three superheroes and a goddess stare at you wasn't exactly fun.

"Nope," they all said.

I paced around my therapist room for a moment.

"Wait," Natalia said. "No one here recognises him, but he was a user of the website,"

Jack stepped forward. "Remember we only targeted active users of the site. I doubt a person who used the site once would have been added to our list of targets,"

I nodded. I completely agreed and considering superheroes had amazingly good memories I believed that no one saw him.

Natalia focused on Richard and her stunning dark eyes glowed gold. Me, James and the love birds also focused on Richard.

A moment later I was coursing through his mind with the others and hundreds of mental images of memories flew past.

We were all looking for the very command that was making this poor man hurt himself for no reason. It was so strange that a god, goddess or superhero would do such a thing.

The deeper and deeper we got into his mind the more I realised how innocent he actually was, and if his memories were correct (which I believed they were) I was impressed with how many sexist pigs he had punched in an effort to save women.

But his acts of heroism didn't stop there.

He defended blacks, gays and transpeople, even though his own opinion about transgender people wasn't completely made up yet. It was so interesting that Richard wanted to defend so many people despite the personal risk.

Then I slowed down inside Richard's mind and everything turned bright white. I clicked my fingers and the others appeared.

"What if this is about who Richard was before all this?" I asked.

Jack and Aiden looked at each other.

"Makes sense," Jack said. "Especially cos Aiden found a newer more powerful command that gives Richard an intense headache whenever he desires to help someone,"

Natalia frowned and our white surroundings dimmed slightly because of her rage.

"We need to find out who put the command in," Natalia said.

"Let's focus on removing it first," I said.

Everyone nodded and we went off coursing through Richard's mind again.

A few minutes later we found the commands in the deepest darkest depths of his mind. The commands were like a massive shadowy ball of oil that kept churning, splattering and tightening on itself like it was choking Richard inside out.

These commands were meant to kill him eventually.

The shadowy ball was inside an immense spherical chamber made from pure black evil with the walls having a slight shine to them.

"Do not touch anything," Natalia said firmly.

I wasn't going to argue.

"Everyone. Activate your suggestion superpowers," Natalia said.

Natalia's eyes glowed intense white as she focused on the shadowy balls, me, James and the love birds raised our arms and white light shot out.

Hissing filled the air as the white light coated and burned and killed the shadowy ball.

Then it started to grow bigger.

It was getting closer. I focused all my energy on my light. It got brighter.

The shadowy ball kept growing.

Natalia screamed in pain.

Us superheroes focused more.

The ball was slowing.

Aiden collapsed.

We focused more.

I screamed in agony.

The ball grew faster.

And faster.

It was so close.

James collapsed.

Jack collapsed.

Blood ran down Natalia's face.

I screamed.

I charged towards the shadowy ball.

Launching everything I had at it.

The ball shrieked.

It screamed.

It melted.

It disappeared.

Natalia slowly laughed before she collapsed and then I found myself still frozen in time back in my therapist room with three superheroes and a Goddess unconscious around me.

Something a very horny woman who just saved a man could definitely take advantage of.

But I won't.

***

Thankfully it didn't take Natalia, James and Jack too long to recover, and it was great knowing they were okay. Then I simply tricked Richard into believing the two hours had flown by and he had had a blast with me.

He was always going to believe it but I did use my superpowers to make him really, really believe it.

It took Aiden a bit longer to recover but as all five of us sat on my wide range of chairs, I couldn't deny it was great to help someone with my favourite superheroes and Goddess.

But what really concerned me, I had dealt with rogue commands for decades back in the 1940s (yes I am that old. No I don't look over 30) and they never actively attacked you like that shadowy ball did.

Whoever had gone rogue and wanted to kill Richard was an extremely powerful and angry superhero or God.

"You still thinking about the ball," Jack said to me.

Aiden smiled and Jack playfully hit him.

I hadn't realised how deep in thought I was, but it was great smelling the hints of lavender, jasmine and soothing orange starting to fill my office again.

"I am," I said, "I just don't know who we're dealing with,"

Natalia kept frowning. "No offense. I do not believe a superhero did this,"

The rest of us could only nod. The idea of a God or Goddess

going rogue like this was awful, it was rather impossible to think about. But the evidence was clear.

"Let me do some investigating and I'll be back in a few days, weeks or months. Well done all of you today. Especially you Matilda," Natalia said.

I just looked at her. "Be careful,"

She smiled at me and nodded. Then she just disappeared. Leaving my large therapist room feeling very quiet, empty and troubled.

Jack and Aiden stood up holding hands.

"Still on for drinks?" Jack asked me.

I had completely forgotten about me going out tonight, I still had my paperwork and admin to do, but after a day like this where I had saved an innocent person, found evidence of a rogue god or Goddess and almost lost my best friends. I could seriously use a drink.

So with James joining us too, all four of us quickly left my practice and went off to a local bar.

And after all the chaos from the past few hours, I just knew this was going to be a wonderful end to a very interesting day.

AUTHOR OF THE CITY OF ASSASSINS URBAN FANTASY SERIES

# CONNOR WHITELEY

# ONCE TRUST IS BROKEN

A MATILDA PLUM FANTASY SHORT STORY

# ONCE TRUST IS BROKEN

I have always been a rather trusting person, my parents used to say I trusted far too easily and I would probably be kidnapped sooner or later, not that they would care too much, but thankfully I wasn't.

To me trust is something so vital, precious and critical to everyday life that I always encourage and want people to trust me. And when I see people who can't easily trust others I always want to help them.

You could probably call it a compulsion in a way.

My name is Matilda Plum, a superhero in the counselling, therapy and psychology sector so I travel around helping people, improving lives and making sure everyone's mental health is positive.

And that's why I care so much about trust, because as a superhero psychologist and therapist, I need people to trust me so I can help them with what they need. Thankfully I have a superpower that helps people trust me, but I'm so naturally good at what I do, I rarely need to use that superpower.

I'm really grateful people trust me enough for that.

As it was a Saturday morning on a hot summer day with the air definitely feeling warm, but not too hot nor cold, I was walking through towards Canterbury train station with its small brick station building and large archway you need to walk under to get to the ticket machines and by extension the platform.

Originally my plan was to travel up to London for the day, go to a psychology conference for the next week and see who I can help in the evenings, but I just had that feeling that my plans weren't going to go quite as easy as that.

The air smelt wonderful with hints of bitter coffee, sugary

doughnuts with a subtle hint of petrol from nearby cars. It actually wasn't a bad smell and it only made me more excited about my day ahead, but I could feel that something was slightly wrong with the air.

Normally when people are in distress, experiencing psychological difficulties or entering danger, my superpowers immediately pull me in that direction. But this time I was sort of just left wondering what was going on.

I kept walking towards the train station, listening to the trains come and go from the station, people talking and panicking about missing their trains and a few trumpets playing wonderfully from nearby musicians.

It was when I got to the large archway of the train station when I sensed someone close to me was in distress, so I turned around and saw a very young woman standing about ten, twenty metres from me.

The woman was leaning against the train station and the wire fence that stopped people from climbing onto the railway (stupid people as I called them), she looked like she was trying to be invisible but she was clearly upset.

From what I could see, she didn't look homeless or broke or anything. She wore skin-tight jeans, a white blouse with some high heels. Personally I felt like she was given off more young office worker vibes than homeless or runaway woman.

Yet I could be wrong.

Of course I knew I had to go over and talk to her, try to help her and then get on my way to my conference. But in my tacky jeans, black t-shirt and with my dark, dark purple hair, I almost felt embarrassed to go and talk to her.

And for the record, these are my -just-travelling clothes, once I got to my hotel I would change into something more professional to go to the conference.

Thankfully as a superhero of the counselling, therapy and psychology sector, all the myths about psychologists were my superpowers, so all I needed to do was get her to talk to me and I could analyse everything that had happened to her.

I went over to her and smiled.

"You okay?" I asked.

She just turned away from me.

"You look a bit upset. Thought I would check in on you," I said.

She huffed.

In case she wasn't too trusting of strangers, which I could partly agree with and see the logic behind, I tapped into my trusting superpower and to my utter amazement it didn't work on her.

I focused all my strength on her, and my trusting superpower flat out failed.

Just in case it didn't work I blasted a very hot middle-aged man with my superpower as he walked by, he simply smiled and winked at me.

My power worked, but for some reason this young woman was impossible to get her to trust me. That had never ever happened before, so I was confused.

Without her talking to me, it was a lot harder to analyse and understand what she was experiencing, but not impossible. The only thing I could possibly think was the cause was this woman had had her trust broken so many times by so many different people. She refused to trust anyone.

And the only way how she could refuse my trusting superpower would be if her refusal to trust anyone was such a core part of herself that she was nothing without it.

This was breaking my heart that this young woman believed she had to do that. It was going to take so much therapy to help her overcome these trusting difficulties that I was really excited.

I really, really wanted to help her.

"Don't trust people do you?" I half-asked, half-said.

"Leave me alone," the young woman said as she stomped away.

I just smiled as she spoke to me and I finally understood what was going on, and I tapped into her mind.

It was actually a really sad story because everyone she held dear had betrayed her in one form or another. Her parents had promised her they would never cheat on each other, then this young woman, Leilani, had caught them both.

Then they both promised her and her brother that the divorce would be painless because they simply didn't love each other anymore and they had both accepted that. But because of the nature of divorces, despite the new No-Fault Law in the UK, the divorce had turned messy, horrid and even hostile.

And to top it all off, both her parents had partners that flat out hated Leilani and her brother. Her brother was only 12 years old and Leilani was 18, so she had to basically raise him with no help from her parents.

I just felt so sorry for the woman.

But I was also starting to understand what I needed to do to at least get Leilani talking to me, and hopefully I would be able to plant the suggestion that her and her family needed to get professional help together.

I could see in her mind how badly Leilani wanted everything to be okay, and she loved her mum and dad and brother more than anything else in the world.

So that's what I was going to do.

I had to make things right between the family.

And I knew that was going to be harder than I ever thought possible.

A damn slide harder.

***

It turned out that Leilani's father and mother did not want to see me whatsoever at their very nice posh corporation offices (same job, different locations) as they both worked with very different insurance firms, so I decided that I was going to have to target one of them and go from there.

I had decided to "go after" Leilani's mother in a way because she was the person who had broken Leilani the most. She was the first person to betray her, break her trust and once she did it she kept doing it.

Thankfully it was hardly difficult to track her down to her favourite lunch spot in all of Canterbury, a very small, cozy and rather wonderful Italian café off the high street. I did enjoy its Italian music playing softly in the background, its cozy little booths and very fit Italian men and women walking around.

For the waiters and waitresses alone I might have to come back here a little more often.

I found Leilani's mother, a woman called Grace, sitting by herself in a booth at the far back of the café. The booth was well-maintained and Grace looked perfectly at home here with her blouse, trousers and high heels.

She looked just like her daughter in more ways than one.

"Grace?" I asked.

She frowned at me but I sat down opposite her. These booths did feel wonderfully soft, cool and relaxing. Yet another reason to return here.

"Who are you?" she asked.

"Matilda Plum," I said extending my hand.

Grace just frowned at me and took out her phone and just ignored me. She was completely rude, so I tapped into my analysis superpowers and I was really surprised at what I found.

I had been assuming that Grace was an awful cheater who didn't mind causing her children distress and putting them through a foul divorce. But it turned out that Grace was in a lot of emotional pain over the loss of her children hypothetically speaking.

Yet I knew exactly why Grace felt like her children were dead to her, because they refused to speak to her.

I couldn't blame them.

"Take it your personal life isn't going so well," I said, tapping into my trusting superpower.

Slowly Grace put her phone away and focused on me.

"How did you know?" she asked.

"I'm good at guessing," I said. "I know Leilani misses you and I'm sure if you just-"

She waved me silent and she winked at the very hot waiter who delivered her some lemonade then went away.

"I don't want to talk to my kids," Grace said. "I have a career and those kids messed it up enough for me with maternity leave,"

I almost wanted to point out how maternity leave had been over a decade ago and Grace seemed to be perfectly okay now, but I didn't. I had to get Grace to admit she wanted to see her kids.

"I know you don't mean that,"

Grace looked like she wanted to fight me but I knew she would crack sooner or later.

"You don't know me," she said, trying to be angry but failing.

"I know you didn't mean to put your kids through the horrible divorce. Tell me, are you still with your affairs?"

Grace just looked in horror at me, I was surprised I didn't need to use any superpowers to make her feel guilty, but there she was looking guilty and like she was about to cry.

I focused on her and made sure she didn't cry. I didn't want her in emotional pain, I just wanted her to acknowledge why this was so hard for Leilani.

"I will not talk to Leilani," Grace said, drinking her lemonade.

"Why?" I said, tapping into my rarely-used truth speaking ability so she couldn't lie to me.

She was really fighting me.

"My... boyfriend will hurt her,"

With that Grace finished her lemonade and ran out of the café, a minute later a very hot waiter walked over and made me pay the bill. I was happy too, just seeing this hot waiter so close was payment enough.

But now I needed to find out who her boyfriend was.

And why on earth he wanted to hurt Leilani.

\*\*\*

In all my decades as a superhero, I have never had to spend so much time replaying someone's mind in my head, and I had to admit Grace's mind was rather dull for the first few hours.

You see, once someone has spoken to me I always have access to their mind (or at least for 24 hours) so it was really easy to find out who Grace's boyfriend was.

"You there!" someone shouted.

I was leaning against the warm metal fence around a massive construction site with massive cranes moving about, people shouting and drilling, and needlessly to say this was an extremely busy construction site where accidents were just a moment of forgetfulness away.

The man walking towards me was a very tall man wearing worker's trousers, a high-vi jacket and a red hard hat. He was exactly the man I wanted to see, because this Leon Jackson was Grace's boyfriend.

"You cannot be here," he shouted.

I just smiled as I activated my superpowers and analysed him. He was about the same age as Grace, clearly loved her and... oh!

I had been expecting him to be abusive, horrible and foul who was demanding Grace never see her kids again. He had said that to her but the context was completely wrong.

Grace had told him about how foul her kids were in an effort to get him to stop asking her to meet them. This Leon really wanted to be part of the family with Leilani and her brother.

"Wait you don't want Grace to not see her kids," I said.

Leon just looked at me. "Of course not. And who the hell are you?"

As much as I wanted to just say *psychologist*, I really didn't want to give him or anyone else for that matter any more reasons to hate me and my profession than more than normal.

"I'm just curious about Leilani. Could you do something for her please?"

Leon folded his arms.

"Could you please pressure Grace into calling Leilani? Leilani really wants to hear from her mother and she wants an apology,"

For a moment there I was sure I would have to activate my influencing superpower to make him do it, but he nodded and smiled.

"Of course," Leon said, then he gestured me to go away. "But please go, this is an active construction site. Don't want you getting hurt,"

As much as I didn't understand how I could get hurt leaning on a wire fence, I smiled, nodded and just walked away.

Hopefully everything was going to work out.

\*\*\*

As I walked back to Canterbury train station in the middle of the afternoon, the sun was making the orange bricks of the station glow slightly, the air was crisp and cool and the only sound around the station was the calm noise of trains coming and going.

I was about to walk under the archway into the station when I noticed Leilani in the same clothes as earlier was still standing in the corner next to the wire fence. Yet this time she was on the phone to someone and smiling.

Really smiling.

The smell of burnt coffee, someone's aftershave with hints of petrol burning made me smile as I focused on Leilani.

It turned out that her mother had called her like Leon had said, he had probably called her the moment I left and now Leilani and her mother were finally talking again. They were laughing, smiling and it looked like Leilani was really enjoying herself.

I analysed her a bit more and I was right, and I was really, really happy that she was starting to trust a tat more. Sure she still had a massive wall around her emotions, but there was a tiny crack in that wall.

So I focused on trusting superpowers on her and when I felt them catch a little on her mind, I gently implanted the suggestion that she should get some professional help. Then because I'm a great boss I implanted the phone number of another superhero who worked for me called Aiden in her mind. At least she could contact him as soon as possible.

Because as I pulled out of her mind, I really knew that in her current state all her friendships, sexual relationships and her life would fail in the end. All because she didn't allowed herself to trust anyone, I didn't want that for her.

As I went into the train station and boarded my train to London, I couldn't be more pleased about helping that poor woman, and now she could finally start to get her life back on track.

And that was really was an amazing feeling, because once trust is broken, it has to be repaired. I certainly understand that a lot more after this case.

AUTHOR OF THE CITY OF ASSASSINS URBAN FANTASY SERIES

CONNOR
WHITELEY

WHISTLER
IN
TROUBLE

A MATILDA PLUM FANTASY SHORT STORY

# WHISTLER IN TROUBLE

I absolutely hate wolf whistlers. There is just no need for such outrageous behaviour and the people that do it are just complete and utter scum.

As I was walking along a delightful little path that ran through the massive campus at one of the local universities in Canterbury, England with large cherry blossoms in full bloom lining the path. All I could hear was the horrible sound of wolf whistling.

I had to get closer and teach the whistler a lesson.

My name is Matilda Plum, a superhero in the counselling and therapy sector, and it is my job to go round and see if people need any help, I solve their problems and I check on their mental health. But I do hate wolf-whistlers.

Thankfully I was walking with my best friend Aiden who was another superhero in the same Sector as me. But unlike my tennis shoes, jeans and a nice blouse, he was wearing some black trousers, a white shirt and black shoes.

He did look amazingly hot and sexy and now I really understood why his boyfriend Jack loved him so much. That was why we were walking through the university actually, because Jack wanted to see us.

As we kept walking through the path I noticed various women started to walk quicker when they passed a very young and tall man.

At first I was rather surprised that he was the whistler considering how handsome, attractive and slightly posh he looked, and I really liked his longish brown hair that was parted to the left. It was definitely smarter than my long hair that I had decided to dye a dark pink today.

With the sound of birds singing, students muttering how much they hated the whistler and the whistling itself getting louder and louder, I just looked at Aiden and he knew I wanted to do something.

Now one of the great things about being a superhero in the counselling and therapy sector was all the myths about psychologists and therapists were actually my superpowers. So people did need to watch what they say, how they acted and how they looked at me, because I could analyse them.

Both me and Aiden stood to one side of the path and tapped into our powers.

As I felt all the hate, anger and rage being directed at these women by the whistler I was just horrified. This man hated women with a passion, and he had… he had beaten so many up over the past few years and that only made him horny.

He always got off on beating up women.

I just looked at Aiden. He had actually gone slightly white.

"We have to stop him," I said.

Aiden nodded. "But there's more. He's part of an entire network of sexist pigs all around the world,"

I really didn't want to believe Aiden so I focused back on the whistler and really focused on him.

"Wow," I said.

I couldn't believe all this, there was actually a website in the dark web dedicated to the celebration, worship and sacrificing of so-called useless women. This Whistler seemed to be someone high-up in the website.

His name was Reuben Grant. I hated his name almost as much as I hated the man.

"We're going to need some more superhero and divine help," I said.

Aiden nodded and bit his lip. I just smiled, I too was rather excited about seeing and working with Jack and my other friends on this problem.

"I just want to deal with this man first," I said smiling.

Aiden started laughing as he could probably guess what I was going to do.

One of my favourite superpowers was the ability to influence people and make them do things they would never normally do, so I focused on the whistler and implanted three simple suggestions.

Firstly he would punch himself in the balls as hard as he could whenever he even thought about hurting anyone (regardless of what gender they were). Secondly, he would call the police and confess to all of his beatings and hate crimes. Thirdly, whenever he remembered and thought and considered his victims or hurting someone he would start crying like a baby too.

"Ouch!" the whistler shouted.

I looked over and laughed as I saw him fall to the ground crying like a baby and he kept screaming how badly his balls hurt.

A woman walked past.

He hit himself in the balls again.

I was laughing so hard I was struggling to breathe.

But me and Aiden had real problems to deal with.

We had to stop his sexist network forever.

***

Before now I had no idea Aiden could teleport me and him back to my very large white office with its smooth walls, high-tech and expensive look.

A few seconds later jack appeared wearing the exact same as Aiden and the two men kissed each other quickly as I sat on my desk, and they sat on two modern chairs in front of me.

If we didn't have massive sexist problems then I probably would have opened a window or something because of how hot it was, but we had much bigger problems than the temperature.

Aiden quickly explained the situation to Jack including the name of the website and his face just dropped.

"The problem is the website is on the dark web," Jack said. "I was treating a guy once who was a depressed computer hacker, learnt tons and he said he liked to own me a favour,"

As much as I hated and refused to let our mental health clients give us gifts, favours or anything else, I definitely felt the need to make an exception on this one occasion.

I just nodded at Jack. He went off and made a phone call.

"What did you want to do with all the members?" Aiden asked.

I grinned. "Well the police will deal with them legally. But I think we should do two things as psychologists,"

Aiden grinned too.

"I think we need to help the victims if any are still alive with their recovery, so they can seek professional help wherever they are in the world, know they do have a life after this and that they're free to live without fear,"

Aiden's grin deepened. "And the second thing?"

I just shrugged. "Let's give the world a major increase in the need for testicle doctors,"

Aiden just laughed. This was going to be amazing fun.

I heard our printer working and moments later Jack walked back in and gave me and Aiden pages upon pages of paper containing the names, addresses and bank account details of the members.

There were thousands.

I really didn't expect there to be so many sexist people spread all over the world.

"It will take us months to deal with all these people," Aiden said.

I looked up at the ceiling. "Natalia a little help!"

Natalia was my boss and Goddess of the counselling, therapy and psychology sector. If anyone could help us, it would be her and considering she was one of the most beautiful women I had ever seen, it was hardly ever a bad thing to see her.

A few seconds later she appeared in my office with her long golden hair, amazingly fit body and just such a perfectly beautiful model-like face. It was no wonder why she was a goddess.

Before she could say anything I quickly explained to her the situation and I honestly couldn't get an emotional reading on her. Her face was like stone.

Now if I was talking to a God or superhero who worked in the gambling sector, then I would have been fine. But considering counselling superheroes and goddesses were some of the most expressive beings in the world, I knew she was furious.

"James!" Natalia shouted.

I was almost a bit surprised she was deciding to call in James Peabody, another superhero in our sector, because I hadn't seen him since I had found him being a creep with his mind reading abilities, but apparently he was a powerful superhero now.

Moments later he appeared and wow! I meant I was leant towards men and women, with men being my main preference, but bloody hell with James in his tight silver suit that left so little to the imagination, expensive haircut and his movie star smile. He had changed so much since I last saw him.

I thought I was about to orgasm. And if that happened I was

fairly sure Jack and Aiden wouldn't be too far behind me.

Natalia quickly explained the situation to James and he had to sit down. All of us hated this network and we were determined to take them all down.

Now we had our superhero and a Goddess team. We were ready. We just didn't know how to get to them all.

I couldn't teleport.

So the problems just kept coming.

\*\*\*

In actual fact it turned out I could teleport, I just needed to have someone actually tell me how, it was a lot easier than I ever could have imagined. Literally.

So as I imagined appearing in number 250 of my list of sexist pigs, I found myself in an awful hospital room with dirty white walls, a large damp hospital bed and a very overweight man laying there, his laptop was still turned-on on the little table next to him, and surprise, surprise he had been typing messages into the sexist network.

The sound of someone crying and wiping away tears made me look at a wooden chair next to the overweight man, and I gently smiled at the crying woman sitting there.

I instantly knew she was the wife of this pig and judging by how blackened and bruised and upset she was, I knew she had been abused terribly over the years.

Out of the 249 people I had dealt with, and healed their families, she had to be the worst affected person.

I slowly went over to her and it was clear as day as she just presumed I had walked in through the door and not teleported in. The woman was wearing long sleeves and I could sense how badly she didn't want me to see the damage.

I tapped into my calming superpower and directed it at her. She seemed to relax instantly and she smiled, it was probably her first smile in years.

As much as I wanted to stick around and really help her, I didn't have the time. I still had another 800 names on my list that I needed to deal with as soon as possible.

I gently placed my hands on her shoulder and tapped into my influencing superpowers.

"Hi there Harper. I need you to do a few things for me, the moment I left this room you will not remember me being here but my suggestions will remain. Understand?"

She nodded. I hated having to influence people this much, as a psychologist it just felt so wrong, but there was no time.

"The moment I leave you will file for divorce, seek professional counselling and you will learn to live with your trauma, going on to live a full productive life,"

She smiled and nodded. I hugged her quickly.

Then I went over to her idiot husband and grabbed him by the ear. He hissed in pain but he was a bit unconscious because of the cancer meds he was on. Sadly he was going to survive though.

"You will let your wife divorce you. You will not resist. Whenever you think about harming another living thing you will hit yourself so hard in the balls you feel like they will break open. You will feel so guilty for the rest of your life about your crimes and abuse that you will cry yourself to sleep every night. Do you understand?"

He slowly nodded.

I wished he would kill himself but my superpowers always added in the command never to kill himself or others. And I liked that.

"Last thing, you will call the police the moment I leave and you will confess to all your crimes. Understand?"

He frowned but nodded and he was starting to wake up.

With that little pig dealt with I just smiled, I had a lot more people to help and I was really looking forward to it.

 ***

About two days later me, Jack and Aiden all appeared back in my office at the same time and they looked exhausted. I couldn't blame them, I felt like I could sleep for decades.

I never knew teleporting, influencing and helping so many people could be so tiring, so as me, Jack and Aiden sort of moved the chairs in my office and half-sat, half-fell onto the warm carpet of my office floor. We all just smiled.

Each of us had helped about a thousand people in the past two, three days and it felt amazing.

The smell of intense coffee filled the office as Natalia and James teleported in, massive smiles filling their faces and plenty of cups of coffee in their hands.

But what surprised me even more was Natalia just sat on the floor as well. Let me repeat, a goddess sat on my dirty floor! I didn't know whether to be embarrassed, grateful or something else entirely.

Yet all five of us seemed perfectly happy as we sat on the ground, smiling and just so pleased with what we accomplished today. Without me and Aiden discovering what had happened, and then the others helping us, I would hate to imagine how many more women would have been beaten and killed.

But thankfully that was never going to happen again.

Natalia clicked her fingers. "I forgot to mention everyone. I got a call from Hippocrates, God of Medicine, Doctors and Biology. He wanted to know why so many of his superheroes were having to treat swollen testicles,"

We all bursted out laughing and I was flat out pleased with all of us.

So as we all just laid there rolling around on the floor of my office laughing more and more about everything, I just knew that I really did have the best possible friends imaginable.

And there was absolutely no group of people I would rather have helping me treat, protect and help people.

No one else at all.

AUTHOR OF THE CITY OF ASSASSINS URBAN FANTASY SERIES

# CONNOR WHITELEY

# THE MIND READING CREEPER

A MATILDA PLUM FANTASY SHORT STORY

## THE MIND READING CREEPER

I fully admit that having to go and get milk is definitely one of the most mundane tasks I do, but there is a very, very particular reason why I do it.

Of course I could send one of my staff off to get such items, I could easily just teleport there or I could do what most people do in this day and age, I could just order it online.

My name is Matilda Plum, a superhero in the Counselling and Therapy Sector, so for me these little jobs like getting milk are just another chance for me to help people. It gets me away from my practice and out onto the amazing streets of Canterbury, England so if anyone is in trouble then I can find them, help them and improve their lives.

Well that's the hope at least.

With my practice being just off the high street with that delightful cobblestone path, tons of university students talking, laughing and musicians playing in the background, normally I would go to a shop for milk on the high street.

But today I wanted to change things up so I was walking along a little street with small well-kept houses lining the entire street, plenty of cars were parked which was normally considering it was the start of a Bank Holiday as it was May Day. Plenty of people had the day off and I had no doubt people would be celebrating their day off later on.

Granted most people would be going to the mini-May Day festival in the high street, I had already noticed tons of stalls setting up with games for the children. I had even helped a very stressed out manager calm down about the event, and I made him realise everything was going to be okay.

It was actually a rather perfect morning, not too hot, not too cold and thankfully not a rain cloud in sight. Which for England was probably as strange as it could get and there wasn't another person out on the street, so it was relatively silent.

And considering I spent most of my days listening and helping people with their difficulties and their conditions, I had always learnt to love the quiet times in my life.

"She's banging," I heard someone say.

Now if I wasn't the only person on the entire street then I wouldn't have been quite as disturbed as I was. But I looked around again and I was the only person out here.

Then I realised that my superpowers had picked up someone saying that, or thinking that, towards another person. And if my superpowers were getting concerned about what that person had said then I needed to check it out.

Thankfully I knew my two staff members, Aiden and Jack, at my practice, also superheroes, wouldn't mind a lack of milk for a little while.

I crossed the road as I felt my superpowers were drawing me towards the high street once again and that was strange in itself. The festivals didn't start until later on, barely any of the shops were open and no students had lectures. So there was basically no reason for people to be going to the high street this early.

A few minutes later I got very close to the high street when I noticed a very tall man wearing a long black trench coat, a cowboy hat and boots just standing in the alley I was going along.

I could smell how disgusting he was from here, I doubted he had showered in weeks or months or even years.

Yet that wasn't what got my superpowers so annoyed. I just got the sense from him that he was up to no good and that something strange was going on.

So I walked up to him. "Hi there,"

The man huffed and looked furious to see me. Then he looked me up and down and smiled.

Normally I'm used to this sort of thing because I am sort of rather attractive according to most people with my very thin, but healthy looking, body, my long hair that I had decided to dye a very light blue today, and my small breasts were apparently something people liked.

I felt something try to press into my mind.

I tapped into my shielding superpowers that stopped other people from tapping into my mind, and I tapped into his own mind to see what the hell he was doing.

One of the great benefits of being a superhero in the Counselling and Therapy Sector was the myths about psychologists and therapists were actually true now. So I really could analyse people by what they were saying and their body language and more.

I was flat out disgusted.

This man was such a creep. It seemed like he wasn't a superhero but he had a mind reading ability and he always focused on their sex lives.

The weirder the better for him.

Then instead of watching pornography at home, he would walk the streets reading the minds of people's sex lives and then he would "deal" with those images later on in an alley. Which was probably what I just stopped him from doing.

But perhaps the most annoying thing about his mind reading ability was how powerful it was. I was almost struggling to maintain my mental shield around my own thoughts, he was really interested in what a girl like me did in the bedroom.

"Stop!" I shouted into his mind.

The man fell to the ground, holding his head.

I really did love my influencing superpower, I hated using it but I did love it when I needed to use it.

The man just looked up at me. It was only then that I realised he was nowhere as young as I believed, he wasn't university age in the slightest. He was at least thirty.

"Why are you doing this?" I asked.

The man just smiled. "It's hot. You clearly have some power yourself,"

That really made me curious because I had never met a person who wasn't a superhero with powers. It was strange but there was a minor possibility that this man was a superhero he just didn't realise it yet.

And no one from the superhero world had contacted him and recruited him.

I know from personal experience how difficult it was learning what I was, how to use my powers and what on earth was happening to me. To say it was a confusing time is a massive, massive understatement.

I was definitely going to need some help.

"Natalia need a little help!" I shouted.

Moments later the entire high street fell silent, the creep froze in time and the most stunning woman I had ever seen appeared. As a woman who was very much drawn to both men and women, I cannot deny how stunning Natalia, Goddess of counselling and therapy and psychology was.

I flat out loved her long golden hair, amazingly fit body and her face was so model-like. No wonder she was a goddess.

Even though I had called Natalia twice before in my superhero career, I was still utterly shocked that I was going to be talking to one of the most powerful people in the world.

Power just radiated off her, and it was scary. I doubted I would ever get used to it.

Granted I mentioned the creep and the rest of the high street was frozen in time, it was more like Natalia had slipped us in-between instances of time so it just gave the illusion of time freezing.

"You called Matilda," she said.

I pointed towards the creep. "Seems he has some kind of mind reading power and he uses it to watch the sex lives of everyone walking past,"

Natalia frowned a little. "Have you got a cause or series of causes?"

As much as I wanted to say that I had, I had been too disturbed by his mind to study and analyse him in any great depth. His mind was just so wrong, creepy and twisted that I really didn't want to tap into it for too long.

But I had to.

I focused on the creep and really started to analyse his mind and then I relayed what I found to Natalia.

"His name is James Peabody, married with a wife and two kids. He used to be… a psychology student then he graduated and he couldn't hold down a therapist job because of his sexual appetite,"

How I didn't vomit I didn't know. It seemed like this guy was completely obsessed with having sex, watching porn and just masturbating.

"He wants to stop but he loves it too much," I said as I pulled out of his mind.

Natalia folded her arms and focused on him.

"Is he one of ours?"

Natalia laughed at me. And it really didn't feel good having one of the most powerful Goddesses and Gods in the entire world laugh at you.

"Relax Matilda. He actually is or was meant to be,"

I was just shocked. How the hell was this man meant to be a superhero working for us if he decided to abuse his superpowers like this.

"Remember Matilda. You were confused about your powers at first," Natalia said.

Damn it. I completely forget that Natalia could read my thoughts easily and analyse me.

"I think I need to plant the suggestion that he needs to come with me and stop reading people's minds," Natalia said.

Now I folded my arms.

"What?" Natalia asked.

"He has to be one of the most powerful superheroes I've met. Normally this sort of mind reading power takes a decade or two to develop, right?"

Natalia focused on the creep again and sort of shook her head.

"He is powerful. He could help a lot of people but he will need to focus," Natalia said.

Natalia clicked her fingers and the entire world and sound slammed back into me like a massive tidal wave for the senses. I almost jumped but I just focused on the creep.

"I'm meant to be a superhero then?" the creep said.

I could feel his mind reading ability just to take into Natalia's mind, and I stroked the surface of his own mind and I seriously wanted to vomit at the sexual fantasies he was dreaming of doing with Natalia.

He was just inappropriate.

Natalia grabbed him by the arm and she looked at me.

"Thank you for finding him," she said. "When I train him up, he could save and help and treat thousands of people, and that's all because of you,"

And with that they vanished.

76

\*\*\*

It turns out I might have completely misjudged the creep, because about an hour later as I was walking back to my practice with four pints of milk in my hand, I got a mental message from Natalia.

I was walking along a little off-shoot of the cobblestone high street with little old coffee shops and other wonders in Tudor-style houses lining the street. It was delightful with the hints of coffee, cream cakes and more exotic treats that I would have to try another time.

It turned out that Natalia was extremely impressed with how quickly the creep had been to train up. Before he fell into his sexual addiction he had been a great psychology student and junior therapist, and thankfully he had remembered most of it.

And I was surprisingly happy about that because it meant he could go out into the world, help people and improve their lives. That was never a bad thing.

I knew that Jack and Aiden would be wondering what took me so long, but they would be extremely happy that I helped someone and finally we could all have a nice cup of coffee together to celebrate.

Because the world always needed more superheroes, I was just amazed and grateful and relieved that I had managed to give the world another one.

AUTHOR OF THE CITY OF ASSASSINS URBAN FANTASY SERIES

# CONNOR WHITELEY

## FINDING TWISTED LOVERS

A MATILDA PLUM FANTASY SHORT STORY

# FINDING TWISTED LOVERS

Bloody hell, let me tell you being a superhero on a very drunk night out is amazing. Not only can you drink a lot, lot more before you start to be seriously drunk but you get no hangover the next morning.

Brilliant!

So as I sat on a very comfortable black chair around a little glass table on the top level of an extremely packed night club. I was definitely starting to feel a little drunk, the night club wasn't moving too much, but I doubt I could walk too much in a straight line.

It was amazingly fun being a superhero and drunk. Especially because my superpowers also went a little… weird let's call it. Like one of my superpowers was to influence people in minor, subtle ways. So when I found an extremely hot guy and wished he took his white dress shirt off.

He did.

And boy, oh boy it was worth the unethical behaviour. His chest and body looked like it belonged to a Greek god more than a real flesh and blood man.

I loved the show.

Yet I do have to admit with the night club pumping loud pop music, drunk people shouting instead of talking and my own superhero friends talking. I couldn't deny my head wasn't hurting.

It was pounding.

And my sense of smell was plain awful, as all the different hints of gin, beer and other alcohol all mixed together to create something flat out strange. I didn't know if I would stay here too much longer without being sick.

The sound of my friends laughing made me smile as I looked at two other superheroes from the same sector as me. Aiden was a really cute young man dressed in a hot white shirt, tight black trousers and some very stylish shoes.

Then his boyfriend Jack was another adorable guy who was basically wearing the same as Aiden just in a different colour shirt.

I always found it amazing how gays always managed to dress better than me in my jeans, pink shirt and blue hair. Granted I changed my hair colour like the calendar changed days, but I needed a hobby according to my friends.

So I choose dying my hair.

As superheroes in the counselling and therapy sector, it was normally our job to look after people, watch out for people in need and manage their mental health. But tonight was something very special because Aiden had just started working at my practice and I loved it.

It was so nice having another guy around besides Jack because my male clients prefer talking about their difficulties with a man instead of me as a wonderfully hot woman.

Relax, I'm quoting some of my clients. I'm not that vain. Ha!

"He's hot," Jack said pointing behind me.

I looked at the guy and it was the exact same guy who I influenced to take his shirt off, and him and his female date were really getting it on over there.

I really wished I could see what the woman was thinking about, feeling and experiencing.

Images of the woman killing, eating and frying the man entered my mind.

"Shit!" I shouted. "Fucking hell!"

Jack and Aiden just looked at me, so I quickly told them what I had seen and despite how drunk they were. They also tapped into the hot guy's and his date's minds and saw what I did.

"Hot guy's also thinking the same," Jack said. "Just not as fucking twisted,"

I quickly realised that the two killers or twisted lovers must have been groaning or talking or moaning to each other, because unless we're touching someone it's the only way how we can read their minds.

I really did love that about being a superhero, all the myths about therapists became true. I really could analyse people by how they spoke.

"What we do?" Aiden asked, clearly drunk.

I just smiled. "Well we are here to celebrate you joining my practice,"

Jack smiled too. He knew exactly how my mind worked sometimes and sometimes I could be a tat twisted myself. Just not quite as much as Jack, and definitely not as much as these two lovers.

"Want to implant some suggestions for tomorrow?" Jack asked.

"Of course," I said almost laughing.

I focused my influencing superpowers on the woman and made her want to be sick all over the man.

She suddenly vomited. All into the guy's mouth, over his stomach and all over his crotch.

Jack started laughing. I did too.

The man vomited too. All into the woman's mouth and into her hair.

They both looked fuming.

We were all laughing so hard no sound was coming out.

After barely managing to recover from laughing, I focused my influencing superpower on making the woman want to get out of there and not kill anyone tonight.

She didn't seem like she wanted to do that. She was fighting me.

I clicked my fingers and I felt Jack and Aiden lend me some of their superpowers so I could strengthen my command.

After a few moments I felt the command sink in and then I did the same to the hot man. He was a lot easier to convince.

But they both muttered something about other victims, and how much of a shame it was that they weren't going to be able to add to their tally tonight.

"There are a lot more vics out there," I said.

Jack nodded and looked like he was focusing on the man.

"Got it. All his victims are buried in his back garden," Jack said.

I focused on the woman and as she was talking to herself, I easily got into her mind and saw where she had buried her victims.

"Got it," I said smiling.

Jack hugged Aiden and they both looked at me.

"Should we really celebrate tonight?" Jack asked.

I just laughed at what he was referring to, so I focused as the twisted man and woman started to walk away, I really focused on them. I wanted them to feel extremely guilty about all the killing they had done and whenever that happened they wanted to confess to everyone around them.

They were already hesitant about that command.

I clicked my fingers, and both Jack and Aiden threw all their energy at me. I loved the feeling of their power, youthfulness and love flow through me.

Neither one of us wanted these monsters to hurt anyone.

The command went through and as me, Jack and Aiden just wet ourselves laughing as we watched those monsters break down in tears and wail, cry and shout about the killing they had done.

It was a hell of a way to end tonight.

\*\*\*

About an hour later the night club was a lot more empty, the music, talking and shouting was quieter and the police had arrived. Me and Jack and Aiden had loved influencing the twisted lovers into confessing to the police, and thankfully they were never going to be hurting anyone ever again.

That damn well felt amazing.

And with the twisted lovers confessing about the other murders too, I just knew that all the other families of the victims were finally going to get justice, and that really was the perfect way to wrap up tonight.

All three of us got up and as I helped Jack carry a very drunk Aiden out of the nightclub, I just smiled at Jack as I felt all of Aiden's horniness just radiate from him. Whatever was going to happen when Jack and Aiden got home it was going to be good.

I was almost jealous.

Yet as we walked out on the cobblestone high street and I heard the police cars drive away. I knew we had all done an amazing thing tonight, and that was just perfect.

A perfect way to celebrate Aiden's new beginning at my practice.

Maybe this was definitely a start to something great, fruitful and exciting.

Actually, that was more of a definite than a maybe. And I loved it.

AUTHOR OF THE CITY OF ASSASSINS FANTASY SERIES

CONNOR WHITELEY

AUTHOR'S
CHRISTMAS
PROBLEMS

A MATILDA PLUM HOLIDAY FANTASY SHORT STORY

## AUTHOR'S CHRISTMAS PROBLEMS

Even since I was born before The Great War I had always loved Christmas and how it had changed over the decades. I loved all the gift giving, the courting and the grand Christmas parties that use to happen last century, and I seriously enjoy the more modern Christmases too.

I always make sure I do my Christmas shopping early in December so it leaves Christmas Eve and Christmas Day free for me to go out and do my job.

And yes, it is a very fortunate factor that I get to work on Christmas day.

But thankfully Christmas Day was only three days away, and I was seriously looking forward to that.

My name is Matilda Plum, a superhero in the counselling, therapy and psychology sector. It is my job and utter passion to travel round helping people, solve their problems and maintain their mental health.

It's a great job and I love it.

I also love that Christmas time is both my busiest and quietest times of the year as everyone is filled with merriment, happiness and all that sense of goodwill crap that we teach children to believe in.

I was walking down a particularly wonderful stretch of Canterbury high street in England with the delightfully cold air blowing gently just chilling my skin enough to know it was cold, but not too much that I wanted to go home.

There were plenty of little shops with Christmas lights, decorative and free samples of mulled wine (I got so drunk going to all the shops sampling their goods one year). And the sound of people singing carols in the distance made me smile.

There was so much goodwill in the air that I loved it, but I was NOT letting carollers stop me, not when I had a job to do. Because in my opinion, carollers are the plague of Christmas, most of them can't sing, they're too bubbly and they won't go away unless you give them money.

I was just about to take my shopping bags, filled with fresh vegetables, meats and other things I needed for my annual Psychology Superheroes Dinner, into a very large kitchenware store (because my friends broke my roasting tins. Don't ask!) when I sensed something.

You see being a superhero psychologist meant all the myths and misconceptions about psychologists are my superpowers, and right now my spidey sense was telling me not to go in the kitchenware store but to go into the bookstore next door.

I looked at the large four-storey high bookstore for a moment with its tinsel, Christmas lights and Christmas displays in the window for a moment. And I did need to grab my friend Octavia, a superhero in the gambling sector, a book for Christmas.

So I might as well kill two birds with one stone.

As I entered the very large bookstore I was surprised at the sheer amount of little wooden tables in rows in front of me filled with brand new books from so many authors.

Then I noticed how the bookstore had ever so carefully created a pathway for readers to start looking at one genre and end up at the same table. My superhero powers were telling me there were so many little tricks here that made a customer behave like the owners wanted, that it was so clever.

Just not what I was here for.

But I did go over to the large table next to the counter to see what book the owners were trying to push so hard. I was rather underwhelmed, I had been expecting something sensational, maybe a romance, maybe a fantasy book but nope. It was only the latest book by a writer me and millions of customers had gone off.

I sneered at the book and heard the young woman behind the tills laugh quietly. I looked up and her and focused on her long brown hair, tasteful green uniform and long pink nails. She looked great.

"Am I not the only one to do that?" I asked.

The woman carefully moved her head in the direction of a security camera and I understood she didn't want to get into trouble and I understood that.

Since the woman had spoken to me, I used my analysis superpowers to learn that she was a very bright woman from a nearby university who just wanted to finish work on Christmas Eve and go home to her family up in London.

Yet she was concerned about whether or not she would have enough money for petrol.

As much as I don't believe that all humans do actually show the Christmas spirit, I know I always try. So I picked up the awful book on the table, went over to the young woman and subtly gave her a £50 note and bought the damn book too.

The woman subtly smiled and thanked me for the money and I was about to leave when she said something to me.

"You know the author's upstairs you know," she said.

My superpowers urged me to go up and talk to him.

I seriously didn't want to because the entire reason why me and millions of others didn't like his books anymore was because his stories were just so repetitive, the endings were rubbish and the author had turned to drugs.

Personally the whole drug thing doesn't bother me because I know he just needs professional people, but given how bad his books were getting. I didn't have time for bad stories, so I refused to read him now.

Yet I am a superhero first. I had to talk to him.

"Thank you," I said to the woman and I went upstairs taking my rather heavy shopping bags with me.

***

It took me another half an hour until I had finished searching the entire bookstore and found the author in a very dark corner of the bookstore surrounded by horror novels that were on clearance.

The author wasn't very tall, maybe five foot at the very most, he wore dirty blue (I think) jeans, a dirty t-shirt and shoes that must have been bought last century.

This really wasn't how I imagined this author looking.

Even though I was in what I call winter clothes wearing some black jeans, a long thick coat and with my hair dyed green (don't ask!). I still looked far, far better.

As I stood next to him, wanting to be sick at the smell of his cigarettes, weed and the musty books around us. I just wanted to help him, and help make his Christmas a little better.

"Hello?" I asked.

The man didn't even acknowledge who I was, I got out the book I had just bought because I needed to double check what his real name was. He wrote under the name Samuel Ratcliff, but it turned out his real name was Sam Jenkins.

"Sam Jenkins," I said.

Again Sam didn't even react to me.

I slowly started to hum a merry little Christmas tune to myself that was charged with superpowers and as it entered Sam's mind. I began to analyse and learn a lot about him.

Wow.

I knew from the newspapers and local news channels that he had had a rough time of late with drugs, some escorts and other things. But it turned out his wife had filed for divorce for cheating on her, he had spent his life saving on weed and his publisher was about to blacklist him from the industry.

And I knew it shouldn't have come as a surprise to me, but he was seriously starting to consider suicide.

Of course as a superhero I had to stop that, but I also had to somehow improve his life.

"Your wife isn't happy then," I said.

Sam slowly turned to face me. "How do you know? Did my publisher send you? I told them I don't want to write another fantasy mystery book,"

That was what I could use to help him.

"I am… a friend Sam, I was a reader actually,"

"Was?" Sam said.

I knew how upset he was knowing he had lost readers, but his emotion was so raw, painful and he wasn't happy in the slightest.

"I used to love your books. In the 90s they were my bread and butter, I would run home from secondary school each day and my teenage self would read a new book,"

It was a complete lie considering how old I was, but it seemed to make him smile.

"I just can't go on. I hate writing. I hate my life. Even my own family hates me," Sam said.

And that was my path to helping him, I loved it when my clients (which Sam basically was at this point) basically told me how to help them.

Then Sam started to leave. "It was nice meeting you,"

A dark black aura formed around him, he was about to die.

I grabbed him. "You don't have to do this Sam. You can love your writing again, your fans love you still. Hell, I love you,"

Sam sighed, folded his arms and just looked at me. I knew I had some work to do.

"Please, whoever you are. Just… just let me go. The world will not even notice that I'm gone," Sam said.

I gestured to all the horror books on the shelves.

"People will miss you. Your family will miss you. Your kids will especially. If you do this then there is no coming back," I said calmly.

He really focused on all the books.

"I already," Sam said, "have a legacy. My books will be what people talk about,"

I had to laugh at that. Not very professional I know, but I felt like it would prove a point.

And I seriously had to put down these shopping bags. I was laughing so much the bags kept shaking.

"What legacy is that Sam? People hate you and your books, but it doesn't have to be that way,"

Sam pushed away from me and he started to walk towards the stairs.

I focused my influencing superpowers to make him stop. He did.

"Then the world is better without me," Sam said.

I pretended to start crying. "But Sam! We need your stories. Your family loves you,"

Sam slowly started nodding. "I know you're lying about most of this. I don't know who you are but you can't help me,"

Wow! This guy was not making it easy for me.

I quickly searched his mind to see why his publisher kept making him write another fantasy mystery, and to my surprise they weren't. They were making him write whatever he wanted, it was Sam had didn't want to write.

Not the publisher.

"You really don't want to do writing anymore, do you?" I asked.

Sam nodded. "It's boring, lonely and awful. I want to be with my kids but the rewriting as much as I love it, takes so long,"

Well, I was really starting to feel like I couldn't save him, so I picked my heavy shopping bags up.

From what I understand about Sam Jenkins was a man who lived for his writing, family and probably the so-called privilege that came from being a writer. He didn't want to write anymore, his family didn't like him and he clearly had no privilege left.

So I was going to have to make him do something for me. And it wasn't fun trying to hold some large shopping bags.

Making my superpowers as strong as I possibly could I sent into the deepest, darkest corners of his mind to and see his wife and take me with him.

Sam shook his head a few times then he hissed and looked at me.

"Actually, if you really think I can be saved. Come home with me, meet my wife and know how terrible of a situation I'm in?"

I pretended to act like I might be crossing a line.

"Please," Sam said.

Even I was surprised at the emotional pain in his voice. He really was at the end of his tether and I seriously didn't trust him to drive us home.

So I grabbed him and we teleported off.

I just needed to drop off my shopping bags first.

\*\*\*

One of the best things about a superhero is when we teleport the world becomes blurry to people for a millisecond then it's like we were always there. People aren't surprised or don't even suspect we weren't there a second ago.

Sam thought the same thing.

He knocked on his front door, his wife frowned as we entered and she led us into a very modern kitchen. It was rather lovely actually with its bright copper tones, kitchen island and red and green tinsel hanging from the lights.

Then the little tunes of Christmas playing softly in the background.

"What do you want? You stink of weed," the wife said.

As the two spoke (loudly) I tapped into my analysis superpowers and the wife only confirmed what I already knew. She really did love him, he was the centre of her entire universe and she hated doing this. But as she saw it she had to do what was in the best interest of their children and herself.

Then to edge things along, I implanted the suggestion of Sam getting on his knees and being truly vulnerable with his wife. Something he had never done before, and something she really wanted.

Sam did it immediately.

"Bertice, I love you more than anything else in the world," Sam said.

As Sam continued explaining himself, how he didn't want to be a writer anymore, how he felt so disappointed into himself and more. I had to admit Bertice was an awful name.

After a few moments Bertice knelt down on the ground to, they both kissed, said they would work things out and then she asked him how many roast potatoes he wanted on the big day.

After a quick cup of coffee, Sam showed me on the way out and as me and him stood outside of their house, he asked me a question I didn't know how to answer.

"I don't know what you did, but thank you. I mean it. But who are you?"

"You're welcome," I said and gently kissed him on the cheek. "Happy Christmas,"

Then I teleported away and landed back in my very large, expensive bedroom and I just collapsed on my soft sheets.

I didn't know how to answer that question because I was so many things. A psychologist, a superhero, a saver and the rest. I did so much but I was always the person who was going to help the innocent, solve their problems and protect their mental health.

And whilst Sam might never write again, at least I saved him, and you never know he might write something, maybe something better than before and I really, really hope so.

But my friend Octavia was definitely getting that book I bought. I wasn't reading it, I wanted something new, exciting and different.

And I had a strange Christmas feeling that I wouldn't have to wait too long. Not long at all.

AUTHOR OF THE FIREHEART FANTASY SERIES

# CONNOR WHITELEY

# PREVENTING A LONELY LITTLE CHRISTMAS

A HOLIDAY CONTEMPORARY FANTASY SHORT STORY

# PREVENTING A LONELY LITTLE CHRISTMAS

I needed to help a thief.

Now it is extremely, and I do mean extremely, rare for me to go out and about two days before Christmas in search of emergency mince pies because normally I do all my Christmas shopping five days before Christmas, but it turns out that the entire world has invaded the shops in search for mince pies so I still couldn't find any.

It was just ridiculous, all I wanted in the entire world was to get myself another pack of mince pies so me, Jack and Aiden, my two superhero best friends, could have a mince pie or three each during the festive break.

But clearly the world was conspiring against me.

You see my name is Matilda Plum, a superhero in the Psychology, Counselling and Therapy sector of the world and when I'm not off hunting down mince pies, I help people.

In my search for mince pies I was walking down the top end of Canterbury High Street, a delightfully beautiful cobblestone high street filled with ancient twisted architecture and little shops that I simply loved. Like the coffee shop I was walking past was a wonderful mixture of an old Victorian pub with orange and black bricks and the modern age with its double glazed windows and more modern signs.

And I was partly relieved to see that there were so many other men, women and little young families out and about hurrying about in an effort to get last minute presents, food and drinks.

There was a particular young family that made me laugh because there was a cute young mother running up the cobblestone high street holding and almost dragging a young boy and girl along with her. But they were all laughing, smiling and the young mother was making it out to be some sort of game.

And since I had just spent the entire day with clients treating a wide range of mental health conditions, my superpowers were on top form so the mother didn't even need to talk to me for me to read her mind and I knew that she needed a hell of a lot of things for the big day.

Thankfully, all I needed were my mince pies.

I was about to go into a little corner shop in one of the odd streets that shot out from the high street in search of mince pies when my superpowers kicked in and told me I needed to abandon my hunt for a little while.

I carefully scanned the high street and the sea of people walking and running and even skipping up and down the high street, then I found my target.

There was a young man, maybe 17 years old, were was standing outside a second-hand phone shop looking at the display of the latest smartphones, tablets and a few black laptops were there too.

I slowly went over to him, and let me tell you that wasn't easy as I had to fight my way through a massive crowd of people.

That wasn't fun.

When I got to the second-hand phone store, I noticed that the young man was wearing blue jeans, a checked red shirt that made him rather cute and he might have been looking at the display but his mind was elsewhere.

Sadly because this was a person I clearly needed to help, I needed him to talk to me before I read his mind.

"Hello?" I said. "These are some old phones aren't they?"

The young man shook his head like he had just woken up and he smiled at me. "I'm sorry I was elsewhere. I didn't hear you,"

As soon as he spoke to me I started to read his mind and there was only one emotion that it felt like I was swimming through and it was concern.

I had rarely felt someone this concerned before, even people with anxiety, phobias and more never ever had this much crippling worry and concern inside of them. And the more I coursed through his mind the less and less clear it was why he felt this much concern.

"Are you okay?" I asked.

The young man seemed surprised by the question. "Um, why do you ask?"

I shrugged as I focused on the phone display so he didn't feel like he was under a spotlight talking to me. "You just sort of radiate nervousness and concern,"

The man laughed. "I'm sorry Miss. I'm don't know you and I don't really want to talk about it,"

I started to search his mind again and I got a sense that it was something to do with the grandmother or something. In amongst all the emotion in his mind there were plenty of memories about the grandmother and these were years old but they were all at the forefront of his brain.

He was clearly focusing and spending a lot of time thinking about his grandmother, and it was surprising that she wasn't dead.

It was just a shame that I couldn't get a name otherwise I could pretend she had sent me and try to help the man that way.

"Merry Christmas," the young man said going into the store.

Yet that was a strange thing because I knew from his mind that he had a phone working perfectly and he had already bought all of his Christmas presents for his family, friends and he had even bought a few things for the homeless people around Canterbury.

Why was he going into the store?

I looked through the front glass door and as I was still connected to his mind I was surprised that he felt guilty now.

I instantly knew that he was going to go into the store to steal a phone or sim card but it wasn't something that he didn't *want* to do, he just *had* to do it for some reason.

Thankfully as my superpowers are all the myths and misconceptions surrounding psychologists I simply sent more suggestions into his mind and he came back go of the store and he smiled at me.

"You didn't get anything then?" I asked.

The young man smiled. "You sort of seem like the listening type. Can I, talk to, you please?"

I simply nodded. "What's the problem?"

The young man started to pace around me and I could tell that I had another problem because he really didn't want to talk to me and his mind was probably trying to flush out my influencing suggestions.

He had a massive problem and he didn't want to talk about it.

"My grandmother... she lost her husband this year," he said. "And I'm worried about her. She lives up North and my family... isn't exactly rich enough to drive up to see her every Christmas,"

I smiled and nodded, making sure not to interrupt him.

"Our boiler broke down and flooded our house earlier this week so we have no money left for petrol to see her for a while. My parents are trying to avoid driving just so they can get to work each day,"

I really wished I could help him.

"So I wanted to help her by... stealing a real phone and sim card and sending it to her. At least that way I could video chat with her,"

I just nodded as finally everything was making sense and I could understand why he didn't really want to commit the theft.

He wasn't a bad person at all, he was only a grandson that wanted to give his grandmother a smartphone so they could keep in contact and prevent her from having a very lonely little Christmas.

Now I just knew exactly what I needed to do and how I was going to save this family at Christmas.

"How about you go home and I'll legally set up your plan? I'll give your grandmother a phone for you can video chat with her later tonight?" I asked.

The young man gave me a very weird look. "Who are you?"

I simply shrugged and started to walk away. "A Christmas miracle,"

Now I had to prevent an elderly lady from having a terribly lonely Christmas.

\*\*\*

"Thank you deary. Thank you," the grandmother said.

Thankfully the advantage of being a superhero is that I have access to the Superheroes of Phones, Laptops and Tablets and they were kind enough to give me the very latest smartphone with all the cool features and they had put a "spell" over it so the grandmother instantly knew how it worked.

I sat in the grandmother's wonderful living room up in Leeds and it was so warm and cozy because of her little gas fire with flames swirling, twirling and whirling in the fireplace. I really liked her baby blue painted walls with pictures of her entire family covering them and the entire house was literally Christmas.

Delightful blue, red and green tinsel hung from the curtain poles and around the picture frames and basically everywhere the grandmother could place it. And what really surprised me was that it all worked perfectly.

None of it looked tacky or out of place. The entire house looked so wonderful, inviting and perfect that I simply loved it here, and it was even better that the house stunk of cinnamon, cloves and ginger because she was baking gingerbread men for the old folk at bingo tonight.

Before I came here tonight, I was actually thinking about suggesting with my superpowers that she should move back down south so she was closer to her family but she wasn't lonely, abandoned or anything. She went to bingo twice a week, dancing three times a week and she volunteered at the local school five times a week.

She was a real amazing pillar of the local community and that was something I really loved about her.

"Oh my," the grandmother said. "I sent a text. Oh that is

wonderful darling,"

I was so glad there was a spell on that phone.

"Your grandson is lucky to have a grandmother like you," I said as I took a large sip of the sensationally bitter coffee that she had made me earlier.

"I do love my grandchildren, all twenty of them, and my children of course. I look forward to surprising them tomorrow when I drive down,"

I just laughed because this woman was clearly never alone and she certainly wasn't going to be spending Christmas alone.

The grandmother laughed. "You superheroes are amazing and before you panic, I did have a great relationship with a superhero from… Police sector or something once,"

I just smiled because I loved it when people surprised me and this one certainly did.

"Thank you," the grandmother said, "for helping my grandson and I am really looking forward to telling him all about my life, and video texting him in-between Christmases,"

Clearly the spell didn't work on the grandmother getting the terms right but she was excited and I didn't exactly want to rain on her parade.

"Is there any way that I can reward you?"

I just smiled at the grandmother. "Actually, do you have any mince pies please?"

The grandmother jumped up, rushed off to the kitchen and bought me in two packs of mince pies. We both laughed, hugged and I wished her a wonderful Christmas because I knew with my search for mince pies over, I most certainly was going to have an amazing Christmas filled with food, presents and wonderfully buttery mince pies.

AUTHOR OF THE CITY OF ASSASSINS URBAN FANTASY SERIES

# CONNOR WHITELEY

# WHAT A MUG

## A MATILDA PLUM FANTASY SHORT STORY

# WHAT A MUG

15th October 2022

Canterbury, England

Now I've really come across some right mugs in my time of being alive, and believe me I have been alive for so many decades now and world wars that even I've surprised at some of the people I've met. Then again, I have actually seen some very weird drinking mugs too at times, especially when I come across weird-ass superheroes that feel the need to get creative with their drinkware because they believe, and I have no idea why, that their special mug or whatever gives them power.

When I come across these superheroes I simply shake my head and smile and as soon as they leave, I simply laugh.

Anyway, my name is Matilda Plum, a superhero in the Psychology, Therapy and Counselling Sector so it's my job to travel around and help people maintain their mental health and basically just solve whatever's troubling them, and I swear I will never ever drink out of a mug after this situation.

I was actually sitting down at one of my favourite coffee shops just off the high street. I really love to walk down the high street on a Saturday and feel the rough yet slightly smooth cobblestones under my feet, the nice cool breeze of the autumn air brushing my cheeks and seeing all the amazing students in the high street.

That's certainly a reason why I love Canterbury, there was so many amazing bright young minds that really help to give the city a refreshing hint of life, unlike so many other English cities that to be honest, just feel dead to me.

But I will admit the biggest problem is that because I don't look a day over 30 (or 25 most days) I do get a lot of both female and male attention, so I'm just glad that I like both most of the time.

Like right now as I sit at a smallish wooden round table in my favourite coffee shop I could see two young men up by the wooden bar looking at me, and talking to each other about who should be the one to start chatting me up.

They actually didn't look too bad and the golden copper light reflecting off their smooth milky white skin made them look very attractive, but they were a little young.

Instead I simply relaxed and allowed the cool metal chair I was sitting in to take the full weight of my body as I waited for a friend to show up, and since I had just finished up a therapy session with a wonderful woman with severe depression the few moments of silence before my friend were great.

And it might sound weird that after a great and rather intense therapy session that I liked to come to very busy places, as there were rows upon rows of little wooden tables with tons of people cramped around them, but I like the energy they give off.

Since my superpowers are whatever the myths about non-superhero psychologists are, I can instantly read a person's mind just by them talking, and I can feel their emotions with only a glance.

And it was such a relief that all these people were so happy today, and it was that feeling of happiness that I really needed. Like there were a group of five expecting mothers in matching black t-shirts, long brown hair and some had their nose pierced, and it was seriously nice to feel their positivity pulse through my body.

Even the amazing coffee shop smelt amazing with its strong, almost choking hints of battery-acid bitter coffee, sweet spiced pumpkins and I even saw a few peppermint candy canes kicking up a faint hint into the air.

Now I could easily understand the pumpkin because it was only two weeks until Halloween, but I flat out hated how shops were already starting to get Christmas products in stock. I love Christmas, but seriously, it had just become far too commercialised of late.

"Hi Matty," a woman said to me.

I instantly looked away from the wooden bar area and focused on the very attractive woman in front of me wearing an amazing black overcoat, white t-shirt and black trousers. It wasn't a look that I thought could possibly ever work but she looked beautiful in it, and my throat even went dry on me.

"Isabella Homer," the woman said to me in a very thick Greek accent. "Distant Daughter of Homer itself, the father of Modern History,"

For some reason I just bowed my head at the woman because I instantly knew that she was a superhero from the earliest days and she had had to be kicking around the planet for at least two thousand years if not longer.

I felt like a baby compared to her.

Granted we had only really met a handful of times throughout the centuries but it was always nice to see her, and I knew if I ever needed help in the History sector then I would only turn to her.

That only made her call and want to meet even stranger.

"What's up?" I asked.

Isabella weakly smiled at me and swirled her hand a little and a small black wooden box appeared in front of me.

Now lots of non-superheroes would have panicked if their friend did that in front of me, out of some strange idea that normal humans could see that "magic", but thankfully if any humans did see that they would "know" that the box had always been there.

I tapped into my superpowers a little and tapped into Isabella's mind just to make sure that the box wasn't dangerous. It wasn't so I opened it.

I was rather surprised when the wooden box dissolved at my touch and revealed a very large golden mug without any jewels, diamonds or anything attached to it. There were only a bunch of symbols, words and phrases in a long dead language that I couldn't read.

The mug itself had to be the size of a small plant pot, it was a little big for your morning coffee but I would love my coffee mugs to be this big.

I just had no idea what Isabella wanted with me.

"This shouldn't exist in history," Isabella said. "The language is a version of Latin that never existed in history and the mug has superpowers of its own. Order a drink,"

Now if Isabella was flirting with me that was certainly a way to get my attention.

"Hot chocolate with soya milk and marshmallows please," I said.

I hardly expected anything to happen but when I blinked the golden mug was filled with very warm hot chocolate and little white marshmallows.

"Wow," I said.

"That's the problem and don't drink it," Isabella said. "The problem is that whenever someone drinks from the mug they turn insane,"

As a psychologist, I have to admit that I flat out hate the term insane because it just isn't helpful but as a superhero I've learnt that sometimes the outdated and harmful terms are rather accurate.

"What do you mean?" I asked.

Isabella leant closer to me and she smelt wonderful of hints of coconut, jasmine and lilacs.

"I mean whenever someone drinks from it. They start rocking back and forth, screaming and cursing everyone around them in a language they most certainly did not know before taking a drink and then those people they curse start doing the same 24 hours later," Isabella said.

I weakly smiled and slowly nodded as I realised exactly how she knew all of this and why she was telling me.

"When were you cursed?" I asked.

"Twenty-two hours ago," she said. "Me and the other

107

superheroes and the Gods and Goddesses in the History sector have tried to solve this but we can't. We need someone who understands behaviour and the mind. We need you,"

As a psychologist there were very few things that couldn't persuade me to help someone in need and she certainly hadn't said any of them. And she was right about one thing, somehow this mug and the language it caused was able to make people behave in "crazy" ways?

The only problem was I had absolutely no idea how it worked and if I could reverse the effects.

No clue at all.

***

Since it was well after lunchtime now in the little coffee shop with its copper lighting, small round wooden tables and amazing smells of bitter coffee, there were a lot fewer people inside now. That was something I was rather grateful for because it meant I could at least start to think aloud a lot more because this was something that needed to be solved yesterday.

Or more precisely, we needed to have this solved in under two hours.

"Do you want another drink?" a woman asked in a tight black uniform and I had recognised her from the local university that I walked through every so often but me and Isabella just smiled and sent warm energy into her.

The last thing we needed was her or any other staff members to kick us out for not ordering any drinks and paying our way.

"What do you mean the language never existed in history?" I asked.

Isabella shrugged and pointed to the symbols on the golden mug. "There are a lot of Latin dialects through time and space but this dialect does not exist. Someone added it,"

I nodded. My expertise laid in behaviour, therapy and the mind, not how a superhero or god could add a language into history without people noticing.

"How could someone do it?" I asked.

Isabella smiled as she tapped the golden mug a little more. "That's the problem. No one knows. All the History superheroes, Gods and Goddesses are accounted for and they didn't do it,"

I stood up and stretched my back and it was only then that I realised I really had been sitting down far too long.

"What about someone from the Time Sector?" I asked.

It actually made perfect sense because the superheroes, Gods and Goddesses in the Time sector were a little weird to be honest, and no one could really understand them too much.

My main problem, and please don't judge me too harshly, is because they constantly see the past, present and future at the same time and they talk like it. They can't describe things in an order that I would perceive them as happening in so I hate to say it but talking to them is hard.

Way too hard for my liking.

Which is actually rather funny considering my profession lives off talking to people through their difficulties.

Anyway, I noticed that Isabella was just staring blankly at the golden mug and I even could have sworn that the golden writing was glowing slightly. Like it was talking to Isabella.

I tapped into my superpowers and started coursing through her mind.

I needed to understand what exactly was going on with her and why she was staring blankly.

Icy coldness slowly grew over my skin and I just felt so cold as I realised that her mind was rather empty. It was sort of felt like walking through a ghost town inside her head, there should have been thoughts, feelings and desires in her mind.

But there were none.

Then I felt everything return to her and I disconnected.

"That felt weird," she said.

I folded my arms and really focused on her mind and it felt different. There was still an icy coldness to her mind as I tapped into it but all of her thoughts were there.

I knew that she wanted to go and get strawberry ice cream later on with her boyfriend (damn it. The hot girls are always taken), I knew she loved football and she even loved… darkness.

That wasn't like the Isabella I knew and the more I searched her mind the more strange ideas and thoughts and feelings that I found.

It was exactly like someone had implanted all these ideas into her head without her knowing. And what was even more concerning was that these thoughts were hidden.

The world went silent.

I instantly looked up and around me before I realised there was no one moving and no sound whatsoever.

I looked over to the wooden bar area and the young woman who had asked about my drink only moments ago was frozen in time as she poured milk into a cup.

Everyone was frozen in time.

"I was worried when someone from the Psycho sector would infer," someone said.

I almost started to look around to see who was talking to me but I knew, just knew that it was something inside Isabella's body.

Isabella stood up and smiled at me. And I had been completely wrong there wasn't anything inside Isabella that was causing this.

This was all Isabella's doing.

And her mind instantly locked me out like it was now a fortress of her own making. She had played me very well.

"What is this?" I asked.

"This is me testing myself," Isabella said. "The Psychology sector is the only one that is powerful enough to stop me. The History sector is clueless, the Time sector, the most powerful I must add, is too deluded to stop me and all the other sectors in the world are too weak,"

Isabella took a few steps closer to me and tapped my head with one of her boney fingers.

"But you my psychologist friend are all about the mind," she said. "You have the power to influence and control and order people to do what you want,"

I didn't have the heart to tell her that even I wasn't quite that powerful but she did remind me of one of my favourite superpowers. I rarely used my influencing ability but I knew I was going to need it now.

"What are you planning?" I asked trying to search for a weak point in her mind to influence.

Isabella picked up the golden mug like it was a holy object and she drank the hot chocolate from it.

It was disgusting to watch as she was like a beast. A very beautiful one.

"The Mug speaks to me. Delivers its guiding light and beacon of hope to me. The Dark God will raise once more and I will be its saviour,"

My stomach instantly twisted into a painful knot as I realised I had heard this exact same rubbish before from other corrupted superheroes.

Last month I had stopped two superheroes from using the magical energy in a nation's grief to resurrect a Dark God of sorts and then I learnt that the two superheroes were part of a cult.

And clearly this cult was spreading a damn sight more than I wanted.

I managed to find a weak point in her mind.

I gently sent thoughts into her mind about freeing me and giving up on this Dark God nonsense.

Her eyes glowed black.

I screamed.

My head felt like it was on fire.

I collapsed to the ground. Holding my head.

"Stupid psychologist," Isabella said. "At least I know how to hurt you. Let your superpowers enter my trap and then I will infect you,"

My eyes widened the moment she said that but I felt nothing

enter my mind and I realised that she wasn't in control at all here.

The golden mug glowed slightly as I looked at it and I could feel a burning sensation scratch the edge of my mind. Like warm water was trying to find a crack into it.

I wasn't going to give it a crack.

"You are weak and pathetic and dull," I said to Isabella. "Only a weakling fool would allow themselves to become used like this from a mug of all things,"

Isabella hissed like my words were actually cutting her.

"A mug of all things. Sure it's a good-looking mug but it's stupid," I said.

I felt the burning sensation grow in intensity.

I launched myself at the mug.

Isabella grabbed me.

Tackling me to the ground.

She punched me.

Grabbing my throat. Squeezing it.

The burning sensation grew. I focused protecting my mind.

The sensation grew even stronger. I was failing. My mind was about to break.

I grabbed Isabella's head.

Sending as many influencing thoughts as possible I could.

I commanded her to release me.

She screamed in agony. Blood dripped down her nose.

She finally released me.

I threw her off me.

I jumped up. I whacked the golden mug off the table.

It shattered against a copper light of the coffee shop and time restarted.

I quickly jumped up and send warm happy thoughts into all the wait staff and the other guests as they were all looking at me and the broken mug like I was an idiot.

I swirled my wrist quickly and the shattered remains of the golden mug disappeared as I sent them off to my boss, Natalia,

Goddess of Psychology, Therapy and Counselling.

If anyone knew what had just happened it would be her.

But I already knew that I was going to hate the answer.

\*\*\*

A few hours later, I stood in an unknown location in a long black corridor with bright white crackling prison bars in front of me as I stared down at Isabella.

The long black corridor had perfectly smooth walls, a rough textured ceiling and hundreds or probably thousands of other prison cells lining it. The corridor wasn't very wide and I was almost scared of one of the prisoners reaching through the bars and grabbing me.

But thankfully I assume that the bright white crackling bars of energy would stop that, and the entire place stunk of strong orange-scented cleaning chemicals that reminded me of orange tarts that I've learnt to hate in recent weeks.

I hate it when my favourite bakery changes a good recipe.

"This is where she will remain," Natalia said next to me. I've always loved her long golden dress, her beautiful sexy face and body and her long blond hair that floats in the air.

She really was beautiful and very, very attractive.

I was about to answer her when I realised how quiet the prison was considering how many thousands of prisoners there were. And I even noticed that Isabella in front of me was speaking but no sound was coming out.

"Most of them speak Dark Languages that we can't allow people to hear, even if that someone is just the air," Natalia said. "Whatever this cult is dedicated to the Dark God it's growing in power,"

I just shook my head at that. "Isabella said we're the only sector that can stop her,"

Natalia smiled. "Don't say that in front of the other sectors. They really won't like that but she's right. I've been increasing the power of our sector for centuries in case we ever needed it,"

I was so glad that Natalia was a smart and very sexy leader. "Did she say why she did this and what was the mug?"

Natalia gestured me and her to walk so I followed her down the long black corridor.

"She did it because the mug promised her power. The History sector can manipulate history, add in events that never happened and can erase events from history if they want. But there are strict rules on that so Isabella wanted to change that and become the Goddess of the sector under the supervision of the Dark God,"

I weakly smiled at my boss. It was a sad fact that humans, even superheroes, desired ambition, power and money sometimes beyond all else and there were truly disgusting people that didn't care who they destroyed to get it.

Isabella was definitely one of those people.

"And that mug you sent me is destroyed now but the Dark God made it as a failsafe. Somehow the mug must have gotten past to Isabella and it corrupted her. The Dark God pours his words, malice and hatred for the world into his objects and then those objects transfer those things to the listener," Natalia said.

I smiled for a moment but not because I was happy in the slightest. I still had so much to learn about the Gods and their history but I was learning. I was developing my understanding but I was still concerned.

Natalia hugged me. "I will keep investigating on my end and sooner or later I will have answers for you. Just keep doing what you're doing at the moment. You're doing great,"

Then she disappeared.

As I stood there in the quiet of the unknown prison and I focused on the long black corridor ahead and behind me, my skin turned cold because there was clearly a much larger plot at play here that I wasn't understanding.

But that was tomorrow's problem for sure, and even if the cult or whatever was going on was still active. I would find them and I will stop them at some point because they would reveal themselves once again and then I will stop them forever.

Yet until they did that and sealed their fate, I would return to

Canterbury and continue to help the amazing, wonderful people that needed me because that was exactly what I loved doing.

And I just hoped I wouldn't meet any crazy mugs for a long, long time and from now on I was only going to have my coffee in cups.

After this crazy adventure that seemed like the smartest choice, wasn't it?

AUTHOR OF THE CREW OF ASSASSINS URBAN FANTASY SERIES

# CONNOR WHITELEY

# IMPOSTER WEDDING

## A MATILDA PLUM CONTEMPORARY FANTASY SHORT STORY

# IMPOSTER WEDDING
## 30th November 2022
## Rochester, England

After this case I am so not going to a wedding anytime soon.

Whenever people ask me why I first got into psychology, there is a great range of answers that I give them depending on who they are, of course. If they're a perfectly normal human then I say because it's fascinating, and it is. If they're another superhero and they know that I'm extremely old then I tell them it's what superhero powers wanted me to do and I love it even more. But to my closest friends I say I love psychology because it is absolutely amazing to help people improve their lives and decrease their distress.

You see my name is Matilda Plum, a superhero in the Psychology, Counselling and Therapy sector of the world. So I go round solving problems, helping people and thankfully all of my superpowers are the myths and misconceptions that surround psychologists.

And I'm so glad there are so many myths.

But I have to admit that working in psychology and different people with different mental health conditions, is just flat out weird sometimes and I suppose that it just wasn't until today that I actually realised just how weird things can get.

I wasn't in my home city of Canterbury England today because I wanted to see an old friend in the historic city of Rochester, it seems I have a thing for historic cities mainly because they're absolutely beautiful.

So I had just said bye to my friend, given him a massive bear hug and kissed him lightly on the cheek. And now I was just standing outside of a little wooden coffee shop with a shopfront painted in dark red paint (a colour I didn't really like) with large windows that showed how great, wonderful and cosy the little shop was.

I could have sworn I felt something warm pressing against my mind but after a few seconds it went away. I hoped it wasn't one of my superpowers going off.

That was the last thing I needed when I had a train to catch.

I had had an amazing time with my friend, we had laughed a lot, cried with laughter even more and now I was looking forward to travelling by train back to Canterbury. There was something so peaceful, calming and relaxing about train travel that I was almost excited by it.

That and I had a lot of paperwork to do for my clients so train travel was perfect for catching up.

I was about to start walking up the long cobblestone high street with all its small and large shops either side with their ancient Victorian architecture proudly on show for all to awe at, but I wanted to enjoy the high street for a moment because it had been so long since I last came here.

I loved how the high street was decorated in different amazing shades of greens, blues and reds. Even the people seemed to perfectly accent the buildings in their thick black, reds and dark blue coats.

And I have to admit some of the men and women out today were hot. There was a particular woman with long sweeping blond hair that went down to her amazing ass that I just couldn't help but focus on. She was that hot.

The warming sensation pressing against my mind got warmer.

I instantly knew that something was wrong and as I scanned the high street the warming sensation almost turned burning when I looked in the direction of the cathedral tens of metres away.

I went down the long cobblestone high street, enjoying the bumpy texture under my feet and really enjoying the delightful smells of freshly baked breads, cakes and pastries from nearby bakeries as I went to the cathedral.

A few moments later, I was outside the cathedral's small stone steps that were so worn that I was surprised they weren't a public safety hazard, but all I could see was a bride walking about above the stairs.

But I knew deep down that she was why I had to come here so I went up the icy cold steps, slightly surprised they were cold enough to pulse coldness up my legs, and stopped just when I reached the top.

The cathedral grounds were stunning even in late November with their massive green fields with white frost glittering in the sunlight surrounding an absolutely beautiful cathedral. I really loved the stunning spires that rose so high into the sky that they might as well have been in heaven.

I had to force myself not to awe anymore at the cathedral as I focused on a very fit young woman who looked at the same age I did at 30 years old in a beautiful bright white wedding dress.

The bride looked amazing and she actually looked like the dress was made for her, something I didn't think happened to a lot of brides. And it was even better that the dress seemed to accent her stunning beautiful face even more and as for her long black hair, well, she really was gorgeous.

Then I noticed there was a large wedding party of twenty men in the exact same matching black suit, pink tie and brown shoes that were standing behind her.

They weren't following her, cheering for her or anything. They were simply staring at her.

I focused my sensing superpowers on her and I hated to see that she was terrified but until she spoke to me I couldn't read her mind.

"Excuse me," I said going over to the bride and relief flooded her face.

"Yes," she said. "Can I help you?"

As soon as I heard her speak I read her mind and was shocked at what she was thinking.

Her name was Penelope Lowerbell, a secondary school English teacher who loved her job, loved her now-husband and was really looking forward to the reception in Canterbury. But she was convinced, absolutely convinced that all the twenty men here today were not her wedding party and were in fact imposters.

Now if I was in my therapist office I would probably forced myself not to smile and try to give her some advice and explore those thoughts some more. But I wasn't in my office. I was outside a cathedral on a cold November day and I was concerned about this woman.

"You think they're imposters?" I asked.

The bride didn't even ask how I knew that. "Yes of course. My wedding party never just stares at me. And I don't know where my bridesmaids are,"

I looked over at the group of twenty men again and I couldn't believe it but there were now ten bridesmaids of different sizes in pink dresses standing next to them.

"It's happening," Penelope said.

Of course there was a good chance that I had simply missed the bridesmaids standing there or they had come out of the cathedral when I was talking to Penelope but I knew that wasn't the case.

Something very wrong was going on here.

There was a mental condition called Capgras Syndrome that made people believe their nearest and dearest had been replaced with imposters but as much as I hated to admit it. That wasn't what was going on here.

Something darker was happening.

I turned around. I jumped.

All thirty people in the wedding party were standing right behind me. They were grinning at me like I was a piece of meat.

Penelope screamed.

"Join us Matilda Plum. Join the Brotherhood. Join us Penelope," all thirty people said as one single voice.

I backed away slowly. This wasn't right, this wasn't natural. This couldn't be happening.

I tried to search their minds but they didn't have one. They had a hive mind that was blocking my powers.

All of the wedding party shot out their hands.

Black crackling energy shot out.

I tackled Penelope to the ground. Ripping her wedding dress.

"You cannot fight the Brotherhood of Change Matilda Plum. You cannot deny the rise of the Goddess. You cannot deny the everchanging cycle of Change!" they all shouted.

Damn it.

Clearly it had been far too long since I last encountered this damn cult dedicated to resurrecting the First Goddess that almost wiped out humans, superheroes and the Gods and Goddesses thousands of years ago.

I didn't know what their plan was but I just had to stop them no matter the cost.

"Aiden! Jack!" I shouted into the air just hoping beyond hope that my two superhero best friends would teleport in to help me.

The air crackled, buzzed and popped.

Nothing happened.

The wedding party jerked. Popped. They absorbed into each other until they became a single being.

The being was shadowy black with crackling energy around it.

The being flicked its wrists and ice covered my body except for my head. The being laughed at me.

"My servants have done well Matilda, haven't they?" the being said as if it was behind me.

"Who are you?" I asked as I struggled to free myself.

"I am the First. I am the Woman To Be Freed. I am The Destroyer of The Mantle," she said.

My blood ran cold as I realised I was talking to some form of the

First Goddess. The woman that had slaughtered so many mortals and immortals alike with such ease it was terrifying.

And now she had me.

"The Psychology sector is a dangerous threat to me so my servants created a fake wedding with real souls to feed me," she said.

I looked behind me to where Penelope was meant to be standing but she was nothing more than a pile of ash now.

She had never been real and that scared the hell out of me. I was normally great at telling when people were fake or not but clearly the First Goddess was a damn slight more powerful than I imagined.

I felt my fingers move under the ice. The First Goddess was still weak. I could free myself.

"Jack and Aiden are good people aren't they?" The First Goddess asked. "I want to meet them at some point but they will die before that happens mark my words,"

"No!" I shouted.

I shot out my arms.

Bright white lights shot out.

The Goddess screamed.

She slashed out her hands.

Black torrents of fire slashed at me.

I blocked them.

She disappeared.

Slamming into my mind.

I screamed in agony.

Crippling pain filled my head.

She was trying to break me.

She was trying to kill my mind.

Making me brain-dead.

I focused all my power. I was a superhero of psychology. The mind was my realm.

Not hers.

She kept slashing clawing at my mind. I put up mental wall after wall. She kept smashing them down.

She was getting close to my mind.

My defences were failing.

I felt her laugh inside me.

I screamed into my mind. Pouring all my hate, rage and fury at her.

I felt her shudder in fear. I imagined a massive cannon being aimed at her head.

I fired it.

Then I simply felt nothing more inside my head and I just hoped beyond hope that the First Goddess was gone and hopefully dead.

But if she hadn't been resurrected yet and that was some a weakened form of herself then I seriously didn't want to know how powerful she was if she was bought back from the dead.

I just knew the answer would absolutely terrify me.

*** 

Thankfully I like to believe I have a great relationship with my boss, Natalia, Goddess of Psychology, Counselling and Therapy. I also like to say that she's extremely hot with her long glowing golden hair that floats in the air, amazing hot golden dress highlighting her fit body and a model-like face that I long to kiss, but I don't say these things because, well, she's my boss.

But as I was standing next to Rochester Cathedral staring out over the massive frost-covered fields that were glittering in the early afternoon sunlight, I was starting to question my boss a little as Natalia was standing right next to me without even talking to me.

I know she had scanned me, reinforced my mind and helped to clear out all the junk and suggestions that the First Goddess had tried to implant during her attack, but Natalia still seemed pissed.

The amazing smell of freshly baked bread, cakes and pastries had faded a little since earlier but it was still present and I really did love the smell. It was like a symphony of the senses as the taste of rich buttery brioche formed on my tongue.

Even the wind and sound of Rochester seemed to be dampened by the visit of the First Goddess. It wasn't as loud, happy and people certainly weren't talking as much.

And to be honest that was sort of surprising.

"Have I done something wrong?" I asked Natalia.

Natalia looked around like she had forgotten I was actually here then she smiled one of her wonderful smiles that just filled my heart with happiness. She really was stunning.

"No," she said, "not at all. I'm just scared,"

Well that hardly made me feel better. If a Goddess and one of the most powerful at that was scared, then what hope was there for little old me?

"The First Goddess grows in power each day Matilda. You saw that today and her followers must be getting close to finding her location. They will free her sooner or later and then that is truly the end of everything,"

I weakly smiled at her.

"I will continue my investigations and I suspect that you, Aiden and Jack will continue yours in due course. But stay safe Matilda, the First Goddess seems to be interested in you and I don't know why. Just be safe. I don't want to lose you,"

I hugged beautiful Natalia before she teleported off and left me on the icy cold November day outside a place where people had just tried to kill me.

Not exactly a wonderful place to be.

But my beautiful Natalia was right though, I needed to start investigating this myself because clearly the Gods and Goddesses were not getting very far. And that was starting to be a very dangerous thing indeed.

Thankfully, finding the followers of the First Goddess was definitely tomorrow's problem because I had a train to catch, paperwork to do and people to help. Because Penelope might not have had a mental condition that was impacting her life but plenty of other people did.

And those were the amazing people that I was going to help, support and improve their lives. I love my job and the wonderfully strange places it brings me to and I definitely wouldn't change my life for a single second.

AUTHOR OF THE CITY OF ASSASSINS URBAN FANTASY SERIES

# CONNOR WHITELEY

## SHOCKINGLY BEAUTIFUL ART

A MATILDA PLUM CONTEMPORARY FANTASY SHORT STORY

# SHOCKINGLY BEAUTIFUL ART
29th November 2022

I had absolutely no idea that after today I was never going to be able to look at art in the same way again.

I really should have known when my superhero best friend Aiden had invited me to a local gathering of psychologists that I should have expected something weird. I really should have expected something weird when he phoned me minutes before he was meant to pick me up saying that his boyfriend Jack had surprised him for a romantic dinner for two.

Surprised, my ass.

He was never going to turn up in the first place and I didn't know why I had been set up in a fashion by my best friend.

So you see, I was currently stuck in a massive art chamber with bright white walls, a horrible dark oak floor and tons of tight-suited psychologists that I have never ever met before without a single friend being here to talk to me.

My name is Matilda Plum, a superhero in the Counselling, Psychology and Therapy sector of the world, so it's my job to solve problems, help make sure people's mental health is okay and occasionally save people.

And in case you think all psychologists are superheroes then you are sadly mistaken. I am one of the few superhero psychologists in existence and believed me, it definitely showed tonight because when us superheroes want to host a gathering, we don't pick a posh art chamber in the middle of nowhere.

For the most part, even though I had only been in the chamber for about ten minutes, I really hadn't looked at the art much because art, it just isn't something that screams out fun to me.

Now believe me, I am a very fun person because I have sex most nights of the week with men and women all of legal ages. And I mean I cannot judge when a someone in their late forties takes an interest in me because I have lived for over a 150 years myself and I don't look a day over 30.

I also love being a psychologist and I really do love going to the bookstores and cinema. I frequently buy from the erotica section of the bookstore and wow, I do love a good action film at the same time.

Yes, I am a very complex woman.

But put me in a room filled with suited men and women with art hanging on the wall. This just wasn't my thing but considering I had been personally invited here and I had a feeling that Aiden had signed up my practice (because he also worked for me) to attend. I at least had to walk about for a bit, smile and wave at a few people.

Yet I just couldn't help but feel like something was flat out wrong too.

I couldn't place my finger on it but as I stood in the sea of men and women as they talked, laughed and even sang a little and wore their very attractive black suits, and dresses and the air was filled with the delightful hints of ginger, champagne and nutmeg cookies, I just couldn't help by feel like my mind was trying to force me to stay here.

There wasn't exactly anything that screamed or shouted danger.

Hell, the closest the people in this art chamber came to dangerous was a very elderly man with thick grey hair, who wasn't stable on his feet whatsoever trying to cut a cake with a sharp knife.

Thankfully that was on the far side of the chamber with a long row of little wooden tables with plates, bowls and wine bottles arranged neatly to one side.

At least psychologists were rich enough to get good food, that was certainly a bonus.

"Hi Matilda," James said, another superhero from the same sector as me.

I was shocked to see James here. I had always believed that our boss Natalia, the Goddess of Psychology, Counselling and Therapy, had him working in beautiful mainland Europe.

"Aiden invited me here so I thought I would come," he said. And it was great to see him in a very sexy tight black suit that told me he was very long in their lower regions, and it was always great to see his handsome and smooth face too.

I just nodded. "Looks like the two of us have been made for fools,"

James weakly smiled and I knew why, we had both been superheroes for far too long to know that this wasn't going to end well.

Someone screamed.

Me and James rushed towards the scream.

It didn't take us long to reach a very young woman in a long black dress having a panic attack.

She was on the floor struggling to breathe. She was holding her chest and I knew we had to act.

James immediately got down on his knees and started talking to the woman and trying to get her to respond.

"She isn't responding. I'm calling an ambulance,"

I saw the woman's eyes were starting to grow more distant.

I subtly pointed my fingers towards her and just hoped that one of my superpowers would kick in.

Normally my superpowers came from all the myths and misconceptions about psychologists. That was normally reading minds, influencing people and other things.

I didn't know any myths about helping people with a panic attack. And normally people had to talk to me before I could read or connect to their mind.

"Help me," the woman muttered.

My mind instantly connected with hers because the comment had been aimed at everyone so technically she had spoken to me.

I forced her mind to tell her lungs to open and breathe and calm down.

A second later she gasped and started taking massive deep breaths of the champagne scented air that was a lot stronger here because of the two smashed champagne flutes on the ground next to her.

Now that the woman was okay and hanging onto James, I really focused on her and I recognised her. Her name was Autumn Bloomson and she was a local psychologist that focused on psychosis, she had just finished her doctorate and she was opening a new clinic in Canterbury.

She might have only been 26 but she had done some ground-breaking work on psychosis that could revolutionise the field.

As far as I was concerned she was amazing and I was so glad to help her, but as I was still connected to her mind I could still feel how scared she was.

She wasn't scared of anyone here, in her personal life or anything like that at all, she was scared of what was in the room.

Autumn was scared of the art.

I almost didn't believe it so I checked and double checked that I had it all right and surprisingly enough I did. It seemed that when she had first walked into the chamber she had said hello to people, grabbed some flutes of champagne to give to her friend and then she had seen the art.

Then she had become overwhelmed with utter joy, pleasure and amazement before she became crippled with utter fear.

I had never come across such a case before.

I went over to James and Autumn. I was almost in awe of being next to such a legendary woman that was so amazing, clever and special that I just wanted to hug her, but I had to help her first.

"I need to get out of here," Autumn said. "I can't be around such stunning art,"

Believe me, I am not an art critic or something but this art wasn't so special. Sure on this section of the wall, there were stunning and absolutely beautiful paintings of rich autumn days with thick brushstrokes that really helped the art to come alive.

But I wouldn't want it in my practice.

"Stendhal Syndrome," James said.

I clicked my fingers. I hadn't heard about that condition for a good few decades but it made perfect sense because sufferers of the condition were so amazed and overwhelmed by stunning art that it caused extreme panic attacks.

Clearly Autumn suffered from the condition. James subtly asked her and she nodded.

"Since I was ten I've had this sort of problem," she said.

And I almost wanted to moan at her for making it sound like she was a problem, someone who was messed-up and useless, but no one with a mental health condition was ever like that.

Yet I didn't really want to argue with someone as amazing as her and Stendhal syndrome wasn't exactly easy to help. Especially if I wanted to make sure Autumn still had a career at the end of tonight.

Because as stupid, pathetic and outrageous as it was, there were plenty of old men in this chamber that would certainly be of the opinion that people with mental conditions couldn't be psychologists. Especially women.

And yes I have met dickheads like that plenty of times over the centuries.

"We're going to have to help her our way," I said to James.

He smiled as we both closed our eyes and activated my superpowers and coursed through her mind.

It was amazing to be fully inside Autumn's mind. Her mind was so bright, clever and just awe-inspiring.

It was amazing to see how a person could be thinking of so many opportunities, possibilities and more for treating and helping people with mental conditions all the time. She was currently thinking about a brand-new psychotherapy to help psychotic people.

It was so new and revolutionary even my mind couldn't understand it all but it was so beautiful to look at her mind.

"Over here," I heard James's voice say through the immense networks of thoughts, feelings and emotions that made up her mind.

I followed the sound of James's voice as bright stunning colours of reds, blues and purples shot past me as I coursed deeper into Autumn's mind.

A few moments later I found myself in a very dark spherical chamber with the domed walls made out of black crystal with a single sliver of light coming from the middle of the chamber.

I saw James was thankfully standing next to me.

It was very rare for me to go into someone's mind fully, and I only did it if it was the only choice because some minds were so disgusting that I hated it. And I really didn't want to find something in Autumn's mind that would change my opinion of her.

"This is where the actions towards art are stored," James said as we both extended out our hands towards the sliver of light in the middle.

"Please don't," Autumn said as a ghostly form of her in her black dress appeared in front of us.

I was surprised at her. She really did have a brilliant mind and it was clear that her mind was so intelligent that it forced some kind of mental protection against interference.

I had never encountered a mere human with that sort of power before.

"If you take that ability away from me then I'm nothing," Autumn said. "I don't want to change. I am perfect the way I am,"

As much as I wanted to believe her I was still inside her mind and I knew she didn't believe it. She wanted to change, she wanted to look at beautiful art without the panic attacks but clearly there was a little part of her that was scared.

"Why?" I asked knowing that I was going to have to be a therapist here.

But then Autumn disappeared and the shiver of light grew bigger and bigger and all I could sense was hatred.

"This is not done by Autumn," James said.

I agreed. This could only be done by the work of a superhero or God or Goddess. An evil one at that.

The sliver zoomed towards me.

I jumped out the way.

It shot at James. It caught him.

Burning flesh filled my senses.

James screamed in agony.

I ran over to him.

The shiver smashed into me.

I screamed. Crippling pain filled me.

I shot out my hands.

Bright white light shot out.

James did the same. We got the sliver between us.

Our white light was holding the sliver in place. We were containing it.

The sliver exploded.

Slamming us against the black crystal.

I felt it melt around me. The crystal was going to absorb me into Autumn's mind.

"Natalia!" I shouted.

The crystal stopped and shrieked.

The sliver of light reappeared. I felt its fear. It was scared of my Goddess.

I kicked my legs.

Breaking free of the crystal.

The sliver screamed at me.

I spun around. Punching the crystal. It shattered.

It disappeared.

I spun around.

The sliver zoomed towards me.

It was going to kill me.

I shot out my hand. No more light came out.

Black crystal wrapped round my feet.

I couldn't move. I couldn't fight. I was going to die.

Suddenly a golden woman radiating pure golden light appeared in front of me. She grabbed the sliver and crunched it with her bare hands.

The woman, my beautiful Natalia, hugged me, shattering the black crystal and we escaped from the hellscape that was Autumn's corrupted mind.

*** 

I should have known that something a lot more dangerous was going on than I ever realised when Aiden had told me that Jack had surprised him for a secret romantic dinner. I should have checked that Jack had actually done that, because it turned out he hadn't.

Apparently Jack had believed Aiden had sent him the dinner email when they were both at work. And Aiden believed Jack had done the same, but in reality it turned out neither of them had, so clearly someone had gone to a lot of trouble to make sure I was alone at that gathering.

Thankfully whoever was behind it thought like me that James was still out of the country and in Europe. Thank goodness we were both wrong because it was James had that helped to distract the crowd so no one knew that I was using my powers on her.

And it was James had that summoned Natalia so she had grabbed him first whilst the sliver of light dealt with me.

As I stood in the massive art chamber with the bright white walls and dark oak floor that wasn't really so bad now, I just stared at the stunning painting of a perfectly cold, crisp autumn day in front of me. The air still had hints of champagne, nutmeg cookies that were delicious and ginger.

I felt Natalia materialise behind me and when she stood next to me out of the corner of my eye I wanted to have sex with her right there and then because she looked gorgeous with her bright golden dress, long golden hair that floated in the air and killer smile that was so stunningly perfect.

"Autumn's okay," Natalia said, "I had James take her home and erase her memory of whatever was inside of her,"

I nodded. That was good news. "Whoever was behind this was clever. There were no traces of magic, superpowers or nothing so I don't know what attacked us, or what sector that they could possibly work for,"

Natalia smiled. "That's the point. A Superhero did not do this Matilda,"

As soon as I heard the words my blood ran icy cold and I hissed in pain.

"Autumn Bloomson is a very special type of human. One of her ancestors must have been the abhuman race known as the Human-heroes," Natalia said.

All I could do was nod because that abhuman race were an experiment between the Gods and Superheroes about what would happen if the Gods mixed the DNA of superheroes, themselves and normal humans. It was an experiment to see what the offspring would be like.

Most of them were extremely clever humans with some powers but nothing special. But a handful were very powerful indeed, and that led to a mass killing when all of the Human-heroes had become tyrants.

Clearly one had survived.

"What will happen to Autumn?" I asked not daring to look at Natalia.

Natalia gently kissed me on the cheek and I almost orgasmed as I felt the sheer power, magic and love of her shoot through me.

"She's safe. We'll watch her but I doubt she'll be a danger to humanity. She wants to help it, not kill it. She will always be fine as long as she remains true to herself and her mission," Natalia said.

I could sense that my beautiful Natalia was about to disappear but I gently placed a hand on her wonderfully warm back.

"But it doesn't explain who send those invites to Jack and

Aiden," I said.

She smiled. "There are many things we do not understand about Human-heroes but we know if human DNA is mixed with those of a God or Goddess from the Time sector then dangerous things can happen,"

I quickly realised that Natalia was saying that Autumn had sent those invites for an unknown reason. And as much as I wanted to not believe my boss, I just knew she was right. I had seen people do a lot stranger things for sure.

And there was even a chance that the reason I hadn't seen that in Autumn's mind earlier was because she hadn't done it yet. She hadn't sent the invites back in time just yet, but now she was going to.

Natalia hugged me and my knees felt weak against her wonderful body before she disappeared and left me in the art chamber.

As much as I wanted to phone Autumn right there and then and become friends with her so I could spy on her. I just knew that was wrong and I would become friends with her in the future anyway because we were similar people, loved helping others and loved psychology.

And that was a great way to start a friendship.

As I left the art chamber, I was so glad to be going home and descending into the darkness of the cold November night, because I had saved a woman today from panic attacks, I had learnt something new about a great psychologist and I was really looking forward to what amazing things she would do in the future.

And the future really would be amazing, bright and that all happened because of some shockingly beautiful art. It's weird how life works out sometimes, that's for sure.

AUTHOR OF THE CITY OF ASSASSINS URBAN FANTASY SERIES

# CONNOR WHITELEY

# MANIA
# ABOUT LOVE

A MATILDA PLUM CONTEMPORARY FANTASY SHORT STORY

## MANIA ABOUT LOVE

I certainly think love is a rather crazy thing, because it can make people feel amazing like a drug, it can make people do awful things and it can make people feel things that is simply impossible for others. And believe me, when you've been alive for as long as I have over the centuries, you certainly get to experience a lot of different types of love.

But love is such a strange thing that is very fun to have because you have flings, hook-ups and the real thing. And yet, love is still a mystery for tons of people.

And after this particular case, I was fairly sure love was a very dangerous mystery indeed.

You see my name is Matilda Plum, a superhero in the Counselling, Psychology and Therapy sector of the world, so it's my amazing job to help solve problems, make sure people's mental health is okay and I generally help people.

And surprisingly enough, love is very common for people coming to see me in my therapist office. Be it because of a heartbreak causing their depression, couples counselling or people suffering from psychosis wanting to people wanting to end themselves so they can be less of a burden to a loved one.

As you can see I have a lot of experience on love.

But it wasn't until I was wanting to escape an icy cold late November day in Canterbury England that I truly understood how weird love could be, because me and my superhero best friends Jack and Aiden, the bestest friends I could possibly have in the entire world and they were such a cute gay couple too. And the three of us were simply standing against the massive glass floor-to-ceiling window of a bookstore just off from Canterbury high street.

I had always loved the bookstore with its rather immense gay and straight erotica section that I didn't read at all (at least that's what I tell people) and there had to be at least three hundred erotica titles on the shelves in all their different sizes, thickness and colours.

The three of us were standing by the window because we were really struggling about should we go outside or not onto the cobblestone street in the icy coldness that was only meant to be colder and colder and colder.

Jack and Aiden were all for it because they were in their very cute matching dark blue coats with a faux-fur rim around the hoody. It was almost a shame that they were always more sensible than me and they were even ditching their normal blue jeans for a very tasteful grey jogging bottoms.

They were dressed for the weather. I was not.

Instead I had decided for what I thought was an amazing white silk blouse, blue trousers and white high heels. Clearly the weather was the last thing on my mind and now I was realising that I must have been horny when I made the decision. Because I looked damn well hot in these clothes, just not very warm.

I was about to say we should just teleport out of the bookstore because us superheroes could do that when I sensed something was ever so slightly wrong.

"You sense?" Jack asked.

I nodded and was seriously glad that I wasn't the only person who was detecting something very wrong.

It was sort of a warm sensation pressing against my head coming from the direction of the little cobblestone street outside the store.

I focused my attention back on the window and really focused on who was walking past. There weren't exactly many people outside today because it was too cold for sane people and everyone seemed to be wearing very thick winter coats in blacks, blues and even pinks, now that was a fashion statement if there ever was one.

Then a short woman wearing a beautifully thick coat walked towards the bookstore and she seemed to be constantly checking behind her.

"The woman," I said to Jack and Aiden, before realising we had no idea what was going on and what we needed to do about it.

Thankfully, the woman slowly walked into the bookstore through the very ugly wooden doors and dropped her hood.

I had to admit she was hot. The woman was easily five-foot tall with long flowing brown hair that went down to her lower back and her face was so smooth.

Yet I was a lot more concerned about her eyes. They looked so fearful, scared and like she knew something bad was about to happen.

Jack and Aiden were already halfway to her through the sea and maze of little wooden tables filled with books before I started moving. I must have been too caught up with her beauty, which was very possible. It had been a long ten hours since I had last gotten some lower body action.

That was a drought to me.

When I got over to them the woman was staring at me and Jack and Aiden like we were dangerous or something. Clearly the woman didn't trust anyone and I could feel her only start to get more scared by the second.

"Are you okay?" I asked, sending my calming influence into her mind.

Slowly the woman nodded and then checked back at the wooden doors like they were about to explode or something.

"Yes, thank you," the woman, Janet Jane, said trying to show us she was perfectly calm, collected and happy but Jack and Aiden shook their heads.

Thankfully because she had spoken to us and all of our superpowers were based on the myths and misconceptions about psychologists. We could all read her mind now.

I was shocked at all the thoughts I saw, she was absolutely terrified that a man was about to kill her. The man was named Jeremy Nort and he was obsessed with her after stalking her for months.

And what I was a lot more interested in was that apparently Nort believed the two of them were in a very committed and sexual and serious relationship. Even though Janet was already married.

"Who's chasing you?" I asked.

Janet hissed as she ran towards me. She threw her arms around me.

"Please help me," Janet said as the tears streamed down her face.

Someone pounded on the wooden doors.

"It's him. It's here!" Janet shouted.

"We need to do something," Jack said. "Should we do what we do best?"

I just smiled. "Time freeze,"

Jack and Aiden nodded and with a click of our fingers… time didn't stop.

That was flat out weird. Normally time froze instantly around us when we wanted it and the world would fall silent and still whilst we saved someone. It normally worked whenever we needed it.

It wasn't working now.

The massive wooden doors to the bookstore opened and a very hot man walked in.

This man was hot with his strong model-like jawline, amazingly fit body and it was clear as day that he worked out, a lot.

I smiled as I watched Jack and Aiden give him an approving look but we all had a job to do. I could sense Janet's fear increasing as she hugged me tighter.

"Babe," the man said. "What are you doing? We need to go and see my parents. They would love to see us again,"

Technically the man hadn't spoken to me but because he had been looking at me because I was currently attached to his "girlfriend" it was enough of a workaround for my superpowers to be happy.

I instantly started reading his mind and it was a nightmare. It was so strange to see that his mind was so calm, peaceful and joyous.

The only reason why it was a nightmare was because of all the memories, fantasies and so-called amazing nights of sex that Jeremy had of Janet.

I actually felt so disgusting, wrong and dirty that I wanted to be sick. It was flat out wrong some of the sexual and kinky things that Jeremy wanted, needed to do to his so-called beloved wife.

He was a very disturbed man.

I quickly shared what I saw with Jack and Aiden and their mouths dropped.

"There's no similarities between their minds. They both feel like they know what's true," Jack said.

I agreed. I had never ever seen anything like this before, two people somehow involved in each other's lives but their minds apparently saying that the other was wrong. Janet was saying that she was married, scared and she didn't know this man. Jeremy was saying that she was his wife and loved her more than anything in the world.

"I'm not your wife," Janet said in-between streams of tears. "I have a husband. I don't want to go with you. I don't know you,"

Jeremy weakly smiled. "Honey you know that isn't true. I know my mother is a bit hard work but she loves you. I love you,"

And that was the crazy thing because I was still reading his mind and he truly did love her and he believed everything he was saying.

"Show him a picture of your husband," I said, just wanting to throw out a good suggestion.

Janet shrugged and took out her phone and showed a very hot man who was Swedish by birth and showed it to Jeremy.

Jeremy shrugged. "Oh honey you know that isn't your husband. I'm your husband. That's the cleaner,"

But I instantly knew Janet was the one telling the truth here because I was quickly realising that the photo she was showing Jeremy was her husband on their wedding day.

"Jeremy is the liar," I said to Jack and Aiden.

Jeremy laughed hard. "What? I'm not lying. She is my wife,"

Jeremy took a few steps towards Janet but me, Jack and Aiden all firmly stood in front of her.

Then it clicked.

"He's suffering from Erotomania," I said.

"What's that?" Janet asked.

"It's a condition," I said, "where the person becomes so convinced that a person is in love with that it becomes their reality and they support that belief even when faced with evidence against it,"

"So he's obsessed with me?"

"Yes," Jack said, "and I've worked with people with the condition before and some kill their love interests,"

I nodded. It was very rare for them to kill their obsession and love interests but it happened. But what was more likely right now was that Jeremy was going to kill us so he could get to Janet.

Jeremy flew at us.

I willed my superpowers to freeze time. It didn't work.

I shot forward.

Punching Jeremy in the face. He dodged it.

He slammed his fists into my stomach.

I fell to the ground.

I spun around. Kicking out my legs.

I tripped him over.

Jeremy landed land on the floor.

Me, Jack and Aiden rushed over to him and placed our hands on his head.

"Jack," I said, "have you ever cured and helped someone with erotomania?"

"No the delusions are too embedded in the mind to help but we can change the love interest," he said.

As imperfect as it was and given how flat out against we all were about sending people to mental hospitals it was the best we could do.

And it was the best thing to help protect Janet and any other innocent person.

"Let's change it to this person," Aiden said.

As I felt Aiden send suggestions into Jeremy's mind, I laughed as I knew that he was forcing Jeremy to like an extremely popular and very, very well protected female celebrity in another country. A person that Jeremy could never get to, hurt or anything.

It would be as harmless as we could possibly make it.

"Actually," I said as I added another command into Jeremy's mind about whenever he thought about stalking someone he would hit himself as hard as he could in the balls.

It was just for good measure of course.

As soon as Aiden was done we all got off him and Jeremy looked around the bookstore, at Janet and us and simply shrugged like he had no idea why he had been in the first place.

Then he simply walked away back out into the icy coldness of the November day and hummed a merry little tune to himself.

Then I looked at Janet and used my influencing superpowers to make her forget about this entire situation, Jeremy and anything else that was going to cause her distress.

She slowly nodded as she accepted my suggestions and a massive smile formed on her face like the bookstore was one of the best places in the entire world.

"Goodbye," Janet said as she started looking around the little rows of tables filled with books and I disconnected from her mind.

Me, Jack and Aiden walked out of the bookstore out into the icy coldness but after walking and feeling my mind wipe away the nightmare of Jeremy's mind the coldness was very refreshing. Sort of like it was washing away the dirt and concerns and fears that I had about what Jeremy would do now.

But Janet was safe and at least she could go back to her husband tonight like nothing had ever happened, Jeremy was going to be obsessed with a woman he could never get to and as for me, I was looking forward to a hot long shower to warm myself back up.

And hopefully when me, Jack and Aiden meet back up for dinner tonight, I might meet a cute man and woman for a little late night fun. Because as weird as love is, I actually love the feeling.

Both inside me and out.

AUTHOR OF THE CITY OF ASSASSINS URBAN FANTASY SERIES

# CONNOR WHITELEY

# MISSING GODDESS

A MATILDA PLUM CONTEMPORARY FANTASY SHORT STORY

# MISSING GODDESS

Now I have been a superhero for over a hundred years and I have never ever heard of a God, Goddess or superhero going missing before. Sure some have happened for a few days or weeks but someone has always known exactly where they were in the end.

But my boss Natalia, Goddess of Psychology, Counselling and Therapy, had literally vanished off the face of the earth and not a single human, superhero or divine being seemed to be able to locate her.

You see my name is Matilda Plum and I'm a superhero that works directly under Natalia by helping people solve problems, protect their mental health and I see clients with a massive range of mental health conditions. But I still need my goddess for help and to make sure that she teaches me how to become a better superhero.

I was currently sitting in a massive leather red booth in the middle of London with a large white table in front of me, where, I had taken the liberty of ordering myself and my best friends Jack and Aiden three massive lattes because they had texted me the extremely concerning news. Now we were having a meeting about it and what the hell the Gods and Goddesses were doing about it.

The restaurant that I was in was rather nice in fact, I had never been here before. The walls were covered in all sorts of chaotic pieces of so-called art and awful paintings, but the staff in their cute little blue uniforms were friendly and they made absolutely amazing drinks.

The entire restaurant smelt of sensational vanilla scones, clotted cream and other delightful foods that created a breath-taking symphony for the senses. My mouth was literally watering and filled with the taste of vanilla, I was definitely going to have to get one of the scones before I left.

There weren't too many people in the restaurant but a few older people in their late sixties were huddled around their little white tables in groups. There was one woman that had looked at me a little with wide black glasses, a golden tooth and a half-ripped-off ear but she seemed friendly enough.

A few moments later, the entire world blurred a little as my two best friends Jack and Aiden teleported into the restaurant and sat opposite me.

They were both cute today with their matching blue and red jumper and blue jeans. They were both clearly trying to look comfortable instead of practical but because of the situation I had no idea what *practical* would look like.

I was about to start talking when the world blurred again for a second.

I smiled when another superhero called James in our sector appeared. He was wearing a very posh and expensive business suit and he had probably just been to see clients.

"What's going on?" I asked.

Jack and Aiden held each other's hand.

"It's bad," Jack said. "Natalia has been missing for two days and not a single God or superhero or Goddess has seen her. All the divine beings had a meeting two days ago about the First Goddess problem and that's when she went missing,"

I bit my lip because this was an extremely big problem. For months now we had been tracking down and trying to stop a cult dedicated to resurrecting the First Goddess ever created. Normally that wouldn't bother me but this Goddess was a murderous psychopath (and yes as a psychologist I can say that) and she would happily burn the entire world.

And if Natalia was missing and had been taken by that Cult then they were a damn slight more powerful than I ever could have imagined. And judging by the looks on my friends' faces, they knew it too.

"What are the Gods doing?" James asked.

Aiden wrapped his hands round his massive mug of latte. "All sectors in the world are hunting down Natalia,"

"But they haven't found anything. The Time Sector is even saying there's some evidence that Natalia never existed in the first place,"

An icy chill ran down my spine. "So someone is trying to remove her from existence,"

"Bloody hell," James said.

I could only agree. "If Natalia is wiped from existence then… I honestly don't know how dire the situation will be. Natalia is the Goddess of psychology but that involves the mind,"

Jack nodded. "It is Natalia that protects the minds of humans from corruption, she protects their thoughts, feelings and helps them not to go mindless,"

I gasped as I realised what would truly happen if Natalia was wiped out or died. "If Natalia dies then humanity dies too. Humanity, superheroes and divine beings cannot function without their mind and even if some people survive, if one of them gets a mental health condition then they will die,"

All four of us simply sat there in silence for a moment. None of us wanted Natalia to die because if she never existed then none of us would be superheroes and me, Jack and Aiden were so old in human years, we all probably would have died in the early 1920s.

We had to find her. Now.

"What can we do that the other Sectors aren't doing?" Jack asked.

I smiled because that really was a great question, with a very simple answer. "We're psychologists Jack. We are experts in the minds of our enemies and the behaviour of them. But we are also directly connected to the mind of the Goddess herself,"

Everyone nodded and each of us took the hands of the people sitting next to us to create a circle.

"Everyone," I said, "focus on Natalia,"

We all closed our eyes and I focused on Natalia with her beautiful golden sexy dress, her long golden hair that floated in the air and I really focused on her stunning smile.

Then I felt something within me click into place and I sensed Natalia.

"She's somewhere warm," I said.

"I hear cars," Jack said.

"I sense danger. Fear. Panic," James said.

"I hear Big Ben. I hear news crews in the distance," Aiden said. "I sense Natalia trying to reach out,"

"Come to us Natalia. Come to your superheroes," I said.

"Help me. They're erasing me from time. Come to The Black Dog," Natalia said in a voice that was so faded it was hard to hear.

We all let go of each other's hands but I knew what was going on and I didn't like it. "Whoever has her knew she would reach out to us. This is a trap and Natalia is dying,"

"Exactly," Jack said. "Our boss is dying and we have no other option,"

"Do we call in the Calvary?" James asked.

I shrugged and I looked up to the sky and told the other Gods, Goddesses and Superheroes in the world where we were heading. Just in case they wanted to help us.

I had no doubt that the kidnappers had planted other trails for the other superheroes to follow and keep themselves busy with.

We were alone but as Jack had said we had no other choice.

The fate of the world rested on us.

\*\*\*

We all teleported away from the restaurant and reappeared in a very stinky dirty living room with black mould climbing up the walls, takeaway containers with furry insides littered the floor and the smell of awfully cheap beer filled the room.

I wanted to take a step deeper into the house but the living room was just so awful with its sofa, armchair and broken TV just there. But I did feel like I was being watched and Jack, Aiden and James gestured me to be quiet as they started looking about.

The house was as silent as the grave but the house was warm, damp and exactly like what I had sensed when I had connected to Natalia. Yet the warmth wasn't friendly, it felt... evil or something and that we really shouldn't have been here.

"What's going on?" a young woman in a dirty jumper, mouldy jeans and thick black glasses said as she came through an archway that presumably leant to the kitchen area.

"Who are you?" James asked.

But I waved him silent and did my mind reading superpower. The advantages of her speaking to us and I instantly knew that she was the person who had kidnapped Natalia in exchange for access to a supercomputer by unknown criminals.

The young woman was called Sadie and had a PhD in computer sciences, mathematics and life sciences from Oxford University so she was extremely smart, so I couldn't understand why she had agreed to kidnap and try and kill a Goddess.

"I don't have time for this. I have made a massive mistake and I need to fix it," she said.

"Sadie," I said. "You have my boss. We need her back,"

Sadie looked like she was about to die and she clicked her fingers.

Natalia appeared silently screaming out in agony but her beautiful golden form was so faded and her arms and legs were gone.

"She's being erased from existence," Sadie said. "Some criminals contacted me and wanted me to prove that people didn't control their own minds using maths. I did so and I also proved... I also proved that mental health doesn't exist in maths,"

"You stupid woman," I said. "You are now erasing Natalia from existence and soon everyone is about to die,"

Sadie nodded like she knew this but couldn't fix it. "We only have minutes left until she disappears completely,"

I just looked at the beautiful boss that I had grown to love so much over the decades.

"We need to fix this," Jack said. "We need to prove that mental health and the mind does exist,"

"How?" I asked. "Sadie, was there something wrong in your dataset?"

She laughed at me like I was crazy. "I graduated from Oxford. I do not make such mistakes,"

"No you only make mistakes that will end humanity," Aiden said rubbing his forehead.

"What's Natalia doing?" James asked going over to Natalia that was starting to fade even quicker. "I can't make it out,"

Jack and Aiden and Sadie all nodded the same.

I really focused on Natalia's beautiful mouth and they were right. She was definitely trying to say something but I couldn't read lips. Natalia was trying to send a message and we couldn't understand it.

Damn it.

The more I looked at my Natalia who was now missing her lower body, the more I realised that she was looking at me. And only me.

I held out my hand towards her. "Connect to me Natalia,"

I felt our minds connect briefly but it was such a strange and weak and static connection that I couldn't hear her.

"Implant a thought into me," I said and Natalia weakly smiled.

Natalia's upper body disappeared. Only her faded head remained and I knew instantly what we had to do.

"Sadie," I said. "As quickly as you can you need to hack into the National Health Service in the UK, hack into the National Institute of Health in the USA and hack whatever they have in China and the EU too,"

James, Jack and Aiden laughed as they understood what I was after.

"Then," I said. "You need to add that data into your calculations and that will prove that mental health and the mind does exist,"

Sadie stood there looking unsure.

"Now!" I shouted.

Sadie run off to do as I commanded.

I grabbed James and Jack then Aiden followed me to and I got them into a perfect circle around Natalia.

"Focus on her. Remember what she looks like. We need to slow down her deletion from time," I said.

All of us immediately closed our eyes and truly focused on the boss we all loved. I focused on her stunning face, golden glowing dress and how she made all my female parts flare to life whenever she spoke to me.

"Oh my God! The smell!" Natalia shouted.

We all opened our eyes and all four of us tackled Natalia to the ground by hugging her and she kissed each of us in turn.

I couldn't believe how relieved I felt that I had finally managed to save Natalia with the help of amazing friends.

Then after a few moments of hugging, Natalia leapt up and she just looked at Sadie. As the rest of us stood us we also just glared at her.

Natalia shot out her arm and golden magical energy engulfed Sadie. She started hissing not in pain but out of discomfort as Natalia searched her mind.

Then she simply laughed, turned around and left the awful smelling house. I didn't know what was going to happen to Sadie but she was only a mere puppet in the games of Goddesses and Gods so I doubted anything would happen to her. Well the Gods and Goddesses of Computers might curse her and that was the very least she deserved.

But there were masterminds to find and stop.

And that was exactly what I intended to do now.

***

A few hours later after Natalia, the divine beings and

Superheroes of the Policing and Security Sector raided a warehouse in London, I was most than grateful to hear that all the idiot members of the cult had been arrested, stopped or sadly killed.

The cult had been using the warehouse for months now as their base of operations, they had used it to search all of Europe for the remains of their First Goddess to no avail, and so they had wanted to kidnap Natalia to see if she knew where she was, but Natalia didn't tell them.

And so many of them had paid with their lives tonight. So many traitor superheroes were dead, erased from the official records and left to be as unremarkable to the future as they should have been. All the other superheroes that were still alive would be imprisoned for the rest of their lives and they would never ever be able to escape their prison.

Thankfully, me, Natalia and my best friends were sitting back in the red leather booth at the wonderful restaurant surrounded by the finest, tastiest Italian food I had ever had. My favourite was the crispy, oily and juicy garlic breadsticks that were simply out of this world and even though there were massive pizzas on the table, and a little vanilla scone for myself later on, I was certainly going to savour these breadsticks.

I was about to start talking to Natalia again after finishing a sensational mouthful of a breadstick when the old woman that had been looking at me earlier in the day came up to us. She still looked the same with her thick black glasses, golden tooth and ripped off ear but she *felt* different.

"I presume our little game played out well then Natalia," the woman asked.

And I was just amazed that this woman knew what was going on let alone who Natalia was.

Natalia smiled at us. "This is my beautiful daughter and I'm sorry that a cult got dedicated to you,"

"What the fuck!" me and Jack shouted as everyone then laughed about it.

The old woman laughed. "Yes, I am Natalia's daughter and I am actually the First Goddess, yes I know that's weird but I had sex with a superhero from the Time Sector too many times. And well, my timeline got messed up,"

I was just amazed but it also made perfect sense as to why Natalia had always said she was doing something against the cult but it never seemed like she was making much progress.

"So you created an entire scheme to stop a group of dark and dangerous superheroes from what?" James asked.

I waved my hands around. "You knew there was a large group of superheroes that were turning against you and the other divine beings, so you created a scheme to identify them and stop them?"

Natalia nodded and kissed me on the cheek. My entire body shook with pleasure.

"She's a clever one mum," the old woman said, "and now I must leave you. There's a terrorist attack in Poland that I need to help with. Love you always Mum. Everyone else, always a pleasure,"

With that the First Goddess disappeared and went off into the night and as my best friends and Natalia went back to their conversations like it was just another day at the office (because it seriously was in all fairness), I realised, I truly realised that I couldn't have wished for a better life, friends and job.

Because unlike before I became a superhero, I didn't have a family, many friends and my life was rather pointless. But as I sat around a wonderful table, eating amazing garlic breadsticks, I knew, truly knew that my life wasn't any of those things now.

And I was extremely glad to be in that position and I wouldn't change a single thing in my life because it really was amazing.

AUTHOR OF THE CITY OF ASSASSINS URBAN FANTASY SERIES

# CONNOR WHITELEY

# WERE IN THE WOMAN

A MATILDA PLUM FANTASY SHORT STORY

# WERE IN THE WOMAN

As a child back in the early 1900s, there were all sorts of crazy, awful and terrifying tales to make sure us children didn't do anything that would put ourselves in harm's way. I used to live in the English countryside and would love to go into the deep, dark woods at night but after my parents told me some fake stories about people dying in the woods at the hands of monsters. Well, I quickly stopped.

And even though I've now been alive for over 100 years, it's great to see that times haven't changed too much when it comes to telling children scary stories to prevent them from suffering.

My name is Matilda Plum, a superhero in the Psychology, Counselling and Therapy sector of the world. And even I have had a few cases when a parent or child has come into my therapist office needing help that only I can give them. Which is great because I love helping people.

Tonight I was wearing a very long, sweeping, posh black dress that really highlighted my fit body as I walked down the long cobblestone high street in Canterbury, England. I had always loved the high street's old architecture with fainted paint on some of the oldest buildings, old bricks that weren't used in modern designs and all the little shops looked so elegant despite their age.

And it might have been a rather mild night edging towards the negative numbers, but I did enjoy the cold a little bit. It certainly helped me to feel alive, well and happy to be walking after a particularly long show at the local theatre.

My superhero best friends Jack and Aiden, in their sexy black suits wearing sweet hints of fruity orangey aftershave, were walking next to me with their hands and fingers intertwined, and they were discussing how amazing the show was that he just sat through.

All three hours of it.

How I love the theatre normally, I love shows and I really love watching cute women and men do their business on stage. But when my superhero best friends promised me a magical show I thought it would be, well, magical and not some opera based rubbish with screaming in another language that I couldn't understand.

I'm sure some people would call me uncultured and a bad person but I wasn't because I had stayed through that show without moaning in the slightest to my two best friends that clearly loved it.

Something metal smashed onto the ground.

Me, Jack and Aiden stopped for a moment as we went past a narrow alleyway that was shrouded in darkness. There was no one else on the street, the high street was silent and cold and I knew that something was wrong.

Aiden and Jack slowly edged forward and I followed them as we all went towards the dark alley.

Something else smashed to the ground.

We all nodded as we realised it was coming from the alley and I prepared myself to pull Aiden and Jack away in case something attacked us.

When we looked into the alley we just stared as we saw a very young woman, maybe 19, digging through the grey metal bins eating whatever she could find.

It was even stranger that she looked to be only eating the raw meat that she found in the bins. She was chomping on it as quickly as she could.

The woman wasn't wearing anything remarkable and she looked homeless. Her coat was basically reduced to rags, her shoes were falling apart and her blue jeans were so dirty I almost didn't know the colour.

Yet what was really concerning me was the sheer starvation, not of food, but of humanity in her eyes. It was like she was a wild animal without a shred of humanity left inside her.

"What happened to her?" Aiden asked.

I shrugged because that was the problem. The three of us just knew we had to help her, we didn't know how because all of our superpowers relied on the myths and misconceptions surrounding psychologists, and that often involved mind reading but only after the client had spoken to us.

I doubted this woman could speak.

Thankfully that reminded me of a case I had two years ago when I was helping a severely autistic boy that was non-verbal and the mother believed that I could cure his speech. Of course I couldn't but she still believed in a misconception about therapy.

Maybe that would be enough of one to create a new superpower.

I asked Jack and Aiden if they had similar experiences and they laughed and nodded.

I felt something click inside me and clearly having three cases of the same misconception was enough to unlock or create a new superpower.

"Speak again," I said to the woman and she screamed in agony.

I went to stop the superpower but then I realised she was faking it. The woman could talk but she simply went back to eating her raw meat out of the bins.

"Lycanthropy?" I asked.

I had no clue if this woman actually had the condition that made them believe she was a werewolf but for all intents and purposes it was the best I could come up with.

The woman howled but I knew she was mocking us so that made no sense.

"Why are you mocking us? Why are you eating out of bins? What are you?" I asked.

The woman laughed to herself and chomped on three chicken bones she had found in the bin.

"I was seeking you Matilda Plummy," she said.

A chill ran down my spine. I didn't know who this woman was but she clearly knew me. Something in my experience never ended well.

The woman stood up but she was so hunched, deformed and malnourished that she looked pained by every single movement she made, even breathing.

"I have been searching a thousand years for the person that would become you. Matilda Plummy. I have searched Africa, the Americas and now Europe and I have found you at last my love,"

Jack and Aiden instantly stepped in front of me.

I had no clue who this woman was. I had never met her, kissed or slept with her in all the decades I've been alive. Thankfully Jack and Aiden knew that.

"Do not block me from my love Plummy," she said.

That was something else I couldn't understand. Why did she keep thinking my name was Plummy, it was Matilda Plum not Plummy but if psychology had taught me anything it was that words like that were important to finding out what was going on.

The woman charged.

Jack and Aiden dived forward.

The woman flicked her wrist.

Magical energy crackled in the air.

Jack and Aiden slammed into the sides of the alley.

The woman charged me.

I jumped over her.

The woman spun around.

Grabbing me.

Pinning me against the wall.

She smelt utterly disgusting like a landfill but she was staring into my eyes and all I saw was darkness, corruption and hate behind her eyelids.

I activated my mind reading superpower but I wish I hadn't.

It turned out she was hunting down a warlord from the 1st

century that had murdered her family, friends and entire village. She had eventually found the male warlord and fallen in love with him but he had escaped her prison and went off into the night.

Now the silly woman was obsessed with the idea of reincarnation and that the man would be reborn into another body in another age in another country. And for some reason the woman thought that I was that warlord.

I was hardly impressed.

The woman cackled like the crazy woman she was and she howled into the night and screamed in crippling pain as her skin became fur, her nose became a snort and her teeth became fangs.

I screamed.

I slammed my influencing superpower into her mind. Ordering her to release me.

She didn't. She had a damn strong mind.

The woman opened up her jaw as far as she could. Her jaw was so big she could swallow me whole.

I tried to blast energy out of my hands. I couldn't.

Jack leapt onto her back.

Punching her in the snout.

Aiden kicked her from behind.

The woman released me.

I stopped time but I could see that everything wasn't still and peaceful like it normally was. Normally everything was silent and still and frozen perfectly in time.

But I could see the metal bins shaking and vibrating and they were about to fall over.

My time bubble was about to break.

"Natalia!" I shouted hoping my boss would turn up.

The time bubble shattered.

The woman lashed at me.

She backed me against the wall.

Her jaw shot towards me.

Her breath was horrific.

But I thankfully didn't die as I felt time froze for real around me and Jack and Aiden grabbed me, pulling me away from the crazy werewolf woman we had just fought. And somehow survived.

"Well you don't see that woman every day," Natalia said as she stood at the end of the alley wearing her beautiful, sexy long golden dress that pulsed golden energy and I seriously loved her long golden hair that floated magically in the air.

"What the hell was that?" I asked.

Natalia folded her arms. "She was the First Demi-God, the Lesser Goddess of Werewolves, Corruption and Damnation. Back in the day, if the Gods and Goddesses wanted to punish you we would turn you into a Werewolf,"

"Was that always a good idea?" I asked, knowing that creating an army of werewolves that hated the Gods and Goddesses hardly seemed like a good idea.

Natalia smiled. "Maybe not but I'm more concerned about how the First Demi-God escaped her prison,"

Me, Jack and Aiden gasped and my stomach flipped as I realised what she was saying because we had dealing with a Dark Cult dedicated to resurrecting the first-ever Goddess so she could murder the entire world and plunge all of humanity into an eternal war.

Clearly this was related.

"What about the warlord nonsense?" I asked.

Natalia frowned. "We always believed the First Demi-Goddess was obsessed with a particular man on Earth but we could never prove it. We know she captured someone before we caught her, she kept them prisoner but then they escaped. No one ever saw the man again,"

"Did he have magic or something so he could reincarnate or something?" Jack asked.

Natalia shook her head. "No. No one has that power or magic or ability I'm afraid. The Demi-Goddess was sadly just as crazy of a woman as she always was,"

That sort of just made me feel more and more concerned about the future because it really felt like we were on a knife's edge between normality and utter chaos if the cult wasn't stopped forever.

"I must meet with the other Gods and Goddesses immediately and find out what went so wrong with their last plan to capture the cult completely," Natalia said. "Thank you as always and I will always protect you,"

A moment later Natalia and the werewolf woman disappeared but me, Jack and Aiden just looked at each other in utter silence.

We had all known for ages now that things were moving in the God, Goddess and Superheroes worlds that couldn't be undone but I just never ever thought that the cult we were tracking in our spare time were actually close to achieving their goal. Because surely they had just gotten the location wrong, the cult must have got to find the First Goddess but found the First Demi-Goddess instead.

But what if they didn't mix up the locations again?

I could feel how scared and concerned Jack and Aiden were so I simply grabbed their hands and pulled them out of the alley. The Cult was tomorrow's problem and there was nothing we could do tonight, and the night was still young, mild and possibly crazy so I was going to take my two best friends to the nearest club to see what we could get up to.

And that really would be a fun and crazy and young-way to end a very strange night before we returned to the great world of work, superheroes and hunting down cults tomorrow.

AUTHOR OF THE CITY OF ASSASSINS URBAN FANTASY SERIES

# CONNOR WHITELEY

# CAT SCREAMING DEATH

## A MATILDA PLUM FANTASY SHORT STORY

# CAT SCREAMING DEATH

A deafening cat scream ripped through my bedroom waking me up.

I shot up. My heart pounded in my chest. Sweat dripped down my forehead.

Then there was complete and utter silence and that normally would have been fine except that every single superpower of mine was screaming at me that I was in mortal danger.

The bedroom was in pitch darkness so I couldn't exactly see too much except for the dim outline of my large wooden wardrobe, tons of clothes on the floor and my very large floor-to-ceiling windows that gave me a wonderful view over Canterbury, England with its roman walls, historical buildings and students very close by.

Of course normally I would get up and switch on the lights but my superpowers just told me that moving and not being careful was an extremely dangerous thing to do.

I wondered for a few moments because that scream could have been nothing more than a bad dream but I knew it wasn't. I had had plenty of bad dreams before including ones where I was chased by dogs, demons and aliens but they always felt like dreams.

This did not.

The sound of snoring next to me just made me smile because I had two gays in my bed as they basically spooned each other, and I was rather glad that me and my two superhero best friends Jack and Aiden had gone clubbing last night and they had been so drunk that they had needed to spend the night with me.

I have never been so glad to have them near me, I was about to wake them up when sweat started to drip down my forehead even more but this wasn't a fearful sweat. It was a hot sweat almost like the temperature was rising.

And oddly enough it was.

Outside my bedroom and house, it was a very icy minus two degrees so I had no clue how the hell it was meant to be getting warm for goodness sake so I just knew that I was in deep, deep trouble and not the type of trouble that I normally liked to be in.

I tapped Jack and Aiden on the arm and they both slowly woke up and stayed silent as soon as I placed my finger to my lips. They nodded and silently took off the bedsheets.

I had forgotten that they normally slept naked but it was a good sight so I hardly minded with their seriously fit and toned and sexy bodies.

"What's wrong?" Jack asked, as he wiped a massive drop of sweat off his forehead.

Aiden just looked around but either none of us could see anything strange so I reached over to the little white light switch on the wall. It burnt me.

My hand shot back and now I knew something was extremely wrong. My light switches never burnt me before so something extremely dangerous was going on.

I clicked my fingers and I placed us in-between moments of time so it was basically stopped and I really looked at Jack and Aiden.

"What started this?" Jack asked.

"I heard something screaming. A cat I think," I said.

Aiden shook his head like that was the worst thing imaginable. "Have you ever heard of the Guardians of The Dead working for Anubis?"

I was surprised when my stomach tensed, my body stopped sweating for a moment and my eyes widened. I knew that Anubis was the Egyptian god of the Dead and guarded the entrance to the underworld but I didn't know that he was real.

"Natalia!" I shouted in the air. "Help!"

A moment later my beautiful sexy boss appeared with her long glowing golden hair, massive smile and stunning golden dress that made her look so divine and so damn sexy.

Natalia looked around and shook her head. "This isn't good. Anubis is here and that only means one thing,"

"I'm going to die?" I asked.

Natalia frowned and nodded. "Anubis and their cats never turn up unless someone is about to die,"

"But I can't die," I said like a silly little girl. "I have so many more people to save, more bad guys to stop and… what about my friends?"

"I'm glad we were mentioned somewhere," Jack said. I elbowed him in the ribs for that comment but I really did love all of them.

All stopped talking and remained perfectly still as I watched a little black cat the size of a lion went over to Natalia and sit on my bedroom floor staring at me. Thankfully I could only see it because the golden light shining off Natalia.

"Do you see the Cat?" Natalia asked.

I nodded. I was amazed at how evil, cold and murderous it looked. I knew the cat could easily rip me apart with its immense claws and sheer power inside its body.

I still didn't want to go to the underworld.

"Can you talk to Anubis?" I asked Natalia. "We have stopped a lot of people coming down to him lately and I know he loves us for that. Maybe that can buy us some goodwill and, what do I do about the Cat?"

"I am not a Cat thank you very much," the Cat said in perfect English.

Jack and Aiden came very close to me and hugged me because they probably knew the Cat was talking to me now and Natalia just disappeared.

"What are you then?" I asked.

"How the hell am I meant to know I just know that cats don't look like this," the Cat-Thing said. "I am a slave to the God of Death because of a punishment I'm serving but no one wants to free me,"

I slowly nodded as if this was just another day at the therapist office for me. "What did you do?"

"I…" the Cat said before looking at the ground. "I fell for the wrong creature. I fell in love with a shapeshifter from the underworld and I helped free it so when the Gods and Goddesses found out they punished me,"

Now as a superhero psychologist I've heard a lot of things and I know that you are never ever meant to be judgemental and to be honest I am not. But when a massive cat breaks or teleports into my home in the middle of the night I really think I'm allowed to be a little judgemental.

"Sounds like you deserve it in a way," I said. "Freeing any beings from the underworld is a crime considering how dangerous some of those beings are, but is your punishment over?"

The Cat nodded. "Of course. I was meant to serve a thousand years as this cat being and helping Anubis collect the dead souls of the, well, dead and mourning them as I collected them,"

I felt so sorry for the creature and I was now noticing that whenever the creature spoke it sounded so sad, upset and terrified that its punishment was never going to end. I understood it. I would hate to be surrounded and having to deal with so much endless death for a thousand years.

I went to touch the creature but I backed away.

"I am not allowed to be touched but I do want your help," the Cat said.

"So I'm not going to die?" I asked.

I loved it how Jack and Aiden leant even closer to me like they could actually hear the answer.

"Of course not," the Cat said. "You will not die for decades yet,"

Now I really wanted to be completely relieved by that but considering I had lived for over a hundred years knowing I *only* had a few decades left was a little bit concerning.

"What did the Cat say?" Jack asked.

"I'm not dying today," I said.

Both Jack and Aiden bear-hugged me and it was so amazing to feel their love, friendship and affection flow between us all.

"Can you make yourself seen to Jack and Aiden please?" I asked.

The Cat shook their head and flicked their tail around in anger. Then I quickly caught Jack and Aiden up on the situation with the Cat.

"It sounds like the Cat was curse," Aiden said. "Meaning there is naturally a way to break a curse but that would be hard to find. Who cursed you?"

"I did," Natalia said as she reappeared and I seriously loved her long golden glowing dress.

Natalia waved her hand towards the Cat and Jack and Aiden gasped as they could presumably now see the Cat.

"Natalia my dear," the Cat said, "you look hot as ever but we have a problem still,"

Natalia slowly nodded and I could see the pain behind her eyes. "I cannot undo your punishment because at the time the other Gods and Goddesses willed me to do so. And if I didn't give you an unbreakable curse then they would have, made me suffer the same fate,"

I clicked my fingers. "Natalia a thousand years ago you were a brand-new Goddess, right?"

Natalia nodded.

"So the Gods and Goddesses could have said anything to you and then you would have believed them?"

Natalia slowly smiled and nodded as I hoped she could see where I was going with this.

"So what if you didn't put an unbreakable curse on the Cat? How would you break it then?"

Natalia shrugged and I got off my bed and knelt down right in front of the Cat.

"Why did you say you couldn't be touched earlier?" I asked.

The Cat shrugged. "Because the Gods and Goddesses said if I let a human touch me then I would die,"

I laughed because I knew that wasn't right in the slightest. Anubis and the other Gods and Goddesses of Death might have been obsessed with death and murder and corpses but they actually hated people dying.

I hugged the Cat before it could jump away. "You're safe little one,"

I shut my eyes as blinding white light shot out of the Cat. Jack and Aiden hissed in pain but I felt the Cat change in my arms.

I felt the thick black fur become skin, the whiskers and snout become a nose and the massive lion-like body become all too male for me not to know what I was holding.

After a few more seconds I opened my eyes and was very pleasantly surprised when I saw an extremely hot man in my arms with long brown hair, a strong jawline and very toned body. I mean this man had a six-pack and everything.

Exactly what I liked in a man and his man-tool was very long and thick too.

I stood and smiled at Natalia as she looked so amazed at what I had just done. She gave me a massive hug and gave me such a parental smile because she knew exactly what, or *who*, I wanted to do next.

Then Natalia disappeared and when I had turned around the Now-Human-Cat-Creature was already making out with Jack and Aiden and considering it was my bed, well it would have been rude not to join in the fun.

And even though the temperature was dropping back down to normal, I just had a little feeling that the temperature would climb back up very soon and my floor-to-ceiling windows were definitely going to steam up.

And I'll leave it at that.

AUTHOR OF THE CITY OF ASSASSINS URBAN FANTASY SERIES

# CONNOR WHITELEY

# BUM STEALERS

**A MATILDA PLUM CONTEMPORARY FANTASY SHORT STORY**

# BUM STEALERS

Normally when a former girlfriend calls up and wants to meet with a person they say no, maybe or they say yes so hard that they are basically shouting down the phone at the former girlfriend just so they can prove how much better of a person they are now since their relationship. So when my ex-girlfriend called up apparently needing to talk with me because it was a matter of life or death, well, I couldn't exactly say no but I also couldn't say yes.

Normally I hear about these sorts of difficulties from other people but tonight I was actually sad to experience it for myself. And it just goes to show that sometimes superheroes seriously cannot save everyone.

My name is Matilda Plum, a superhero in the Psychology, Counselling and Therapy part of the world so in normal times I go around helping people, making sure everyone is okay and I help to solve problems. But I never expected to see an ex-girlfriend.

Tonight I was wearing a long sweeping white dress that really helped to show how slim, sexy and fit I was as I sat on a little cold wooden chair in a very posh restaurant in Canterbury, England. There weren't exactly too many posh expensive places in the city because students were hardly that rich, but there were some.

The restaurant was very nice and posh with its massive eating area with brown hardwood floors, massive chandeliers every five metres and crystal cutlery that I was almost scared to touch in case it broke.

The sound of the restaurant was almost deafening with the

constant noises of people hitting plates, laughing and shouting at the poor wait staff. It was a nightmare and I was amazed that I had heard of this place through my business contacts. It should have been impossible to conduct business in such a noisy place.

There were plenty of people in here tonight which surprised me, but I was right next to a window giving me a stunning view of Canterbury Cathedral a few tens of metres from me, and there were two other tables within earshot of me. One table was empty but another had a very cute young straight couple. The man was very sexy with his longish blond hair, evil smile and tight blue shirt, and because I could hear them I just knew that the woman was going to get some action tonight.

Sadly I just knew I wasn't.

Especially as when my former girlfriend, Minty Croftford, had phoned me out of breath, clearly distressed and in need of my help, it turned out that I wasn't mature enough to invite her around to my place.

Instead I decided to invite her to the most expensive restaurant in the city, knowing full well she couldn't afford anything on the menu. Maybe that shouted needy, annoying or insecure but I did not care.

"Hi there," Minty said as she pulled herself out a seat without giving me a chance to even offer. Not that I actually wouldn't have offered I wasn't that sort of person.

Minty was still beautiful despite her ageing dramatically since our relationship had ended back in the 90s, and whilst I still looked the same as I did before World War One because superheroes don't age past thirty, her cheeks and body and legs were rounder and thicker, but she still had a beauty to her that I did miss.

Minty had always been a great dresser and she certainly didn't disappoint tonight with her tight-fitting black dress, massive gold earrings and even larger red lips that were very good to kiss back in the day. But there was one thing that was very, very different about her.

Her bum.

Minty had never really had a bum before and there wasn't anything for me to hold when we were together but now, now it might have been big enough to become an independent island.

That was strange.

The entire restaurant smelt heavenly with hints of garlic, tomato and rich Mexican spices that I loved more than anything else in the world but I was here to do a job sadly and not enjoy the food.

"What's wrong?" I asked.

"I think something is trying to steal my ass," Minty said.

With that little comment, I waved over a very cute young male waiter who was wearing a black waiter's uniform that was certainly too small for him but it looked good, and I ordered me and Minty two diet cokes, three pizzas and one order of garlic doughballs to go. Since I knew that my best friends Superheroes Jack and Aiden wouldn't be happy if I had come here without getting them anything.

"Tell me more about this problem," I said very neutrally and channelling my calming and trusting superpowers into Minty. There were times when I loved my superpowers being all the myths and misconceptions about psychologists.

"I can't," she said.

I leant across the table and gently rubbed her hand as a way to tell my superpowers to take it up a notch. I really needed her to trust me if I was ever going to help her.

"At night," Minty said. "three men come into my bedroom and start playing with my ass. They poke it, play with it and kiss it,"

I slowly nodded and decided that she was either lying or she was telling the truth. So I needed to activate another superpower of mine which involved me reading her mind and thankfully because she was talking to me I could access all of her mind.

As I dug into her mind I was amazed that she was actually telling the truth. It was always the same three men every single night and they would always come into her bedroom at three o'clock in the morning, rip off her clothes and bedding and looked at her ass.

Then they would do all the other things I would do it as well.

The thing that seriously confused me though was that these men weren't men in the slightest. They were humanoid for sure but they weren't men or even human and they weren't even aliens.

They were very earthly creatures called the Greys, and before you even start remotely connecting them to the so-called aliens that live in the middle of the Earth. They are not.

The Greys are very nice, kind and friendly people that look like humans, talk like humans and like to build vast underground empires for themselves unlike humans. Yet I couldn't understand why they would want my former girlfriend's ass.

I was going to need some help.

"Jack! Aiden!" I shouted into the air.

Moments later the entire restaurant froze and the sheer silence of the place made me almost jump but it was good seeing Minty frozen mid-sentence and two very cute superheroes pulled over chairs and looked at me.

Both Jack and Aiden were such a cute couple and tonight they were both wearing matching black shiny suits, pink ties and black shoes. They both smelt amazing too with hints of their aftershaves filling the air rather heavily.

"Opera?" I asked.

Jack nodded. "Yeah don't tell me about it,"

Aiden laughed. "You know you love it really. So what you need Matty?"

I just pointed to Minty and told them about the Grey situation and really hoped they knew something I didn't about the Greys.

"Did you know what her butt implants are made from?" Jack asked.

Normal people might have said no but as I was still connected to her mind I double-checked and was surprised to see that Minty (in all her foolishness) had gone to a backstreet surgeon to have the so-called best implants done and I was amazed that she had only had a two-week long infection.

"Backstreet surgeon called *Smiths Butts*," I said.

Jack and Aiden just looked at each other.

"What?" I asked.

Aiden leant across the table like there was actually a chance of us being overheard when they had both frozen us in time.

"Smiths Butts uses very dark procedures and resources to make the implants. And Mr Smith gets the materials for the implants from a Welsh mountain very close to a Grey burial site,"

"Oh," I said.

And that really was all I needed to know, because if the Greys were anything, they seriously liked to honour, create and be extremely respectful to their dead. I once visited them to help improve relations between them, the humans and the Superhero worlds, and I had visited them during their version of the Day of the Dead but for them it's a Year of the Dead.

I don't think I've ever been as drunk as I was then and I only stayed for three hours.

So there was a great chance that Minty's butt implants contained the remains of Greys, since the bodies of Greys dissolved into sand-like particles, and the Greys wanted their dead back.

I just looked at Aiden and Jack because I had no clue how I was going to tell my former girlfriend what I had found out.

"Have fun," the cute boyfriends said before they disappeared and restarted time again. And it was only then that I realised the entire reason for them stopping time was so they wouldn't miss any of their opera show. I almost felt sorry for Jack.

Minty coughed a little and smiled at me. "What do you think? Can you help me?"

I just had to tell her about the Greys, so I did.

Minty laughed so hard that I thought her face was going to crack. "Yeah right. You really are as crazy as I thought back in the 90s,"

I frowned at her. "I'm very serious. If have dead Greys in your butt then they will kill you for it. the Greys honour their dead very seriously,"

"What would they do to me?" Minty asked like this was all still impossible.

"They were rip out your ass," I said. "They will put their slimy hands down your throat, reach down to your bum and pull your implants out. It's the only way they know how to access the human body as they hate cutting things,"

Minty shrugged and stood up. "You always were good at fairy tales,"

"Just have the implants removed. I know many great doctors that would do it without pain, a scar or anything. Please. Just have them removed,"

I really forced my influencing superpowers to open her mind up to the idea.

Minty shot a look at me like I had threatened to kill her. "Fuck off. I am not having my bum removed! If your Greys want my ass they can rip it off me for all I care!"

Minty stormed around and the entire restaurant was staring at me like I was a criminal.

But I wasn't the one that was about to die.

***

I completely respected the right of a person, any person, man or woman, to decide what they did to their own body. I didn't have a problem with that whatsoever but I did have a problem with Minty dying.

Over the next two days, I had called every single superhero I can think of from the Medical Sector, Psychology sector, Boobs, Bums and Cock Sector (and yes that is a real thing) and all I wanted was someone to give me an idea about how I was going to get Minty to change her mind about getting her implants removed.

No luck there.

I had even showed up at her brand-new house on the outskirts of London with its massive bright white walls, perfectly done rose garden and two immense Land Rovers on the driveway. I had knocked on the door and her wife had hugged me and welcomed me inside and then Minty had kicked me straight back out.

Afterwards I decided I had no other option than to get me, Jack and Aiden to constantly phone her home phone and mobile every minute we had in-between helping our clients at my mental health clinic.

That didn't last more than ten minutes because she blocked all our numbers.

I had even decided to go to see the Greys because they loved me for some reason and I had managed to get them to give me two more days to see if I could retrieve their dead relatives without them effectively killing Minty.

The only option I had left was to be unethical and get the implants removed without her consent but I wasn't going to do it, my boss wouldn't allow me to do it and even if I did do it to save her single life, I would never forgive myself.

Because I have been alive since before the first world war and I have seen first-hand the horrific consequences of people not being allowed to decide what they did to their bodies.

So three days later, after trying to see Minty again and getting shot down and causing Minty and her wife to get divorced because the wife believed me, I sat at my large dark brown desk in my therapist room with a wide range of chairs surrounding me and I read the local paper.

Minty had been found dead at the strike of midnight in her house when neighbours had heard her screaming out in agony and they had found her bedsheets wet with blood and her ass was as flat as it was the day she had been born.

As much as I hated what had happened I couldn't really be angry at myself because I had tried everything over the past three to five days (I had been so busy I didn't even know what the day was) but as I still had access to her mind up until she died because I had never shut off the connection, I gave it a final scan.

And I had found something very, very important.

When I have clients with some forms of eating disorders, self-esteem amongst other conditions, I tend to see that they attach a lot of their happiness to a certain part of their body. And it turned out that Minty was obsessed with having a big ass.

She clearly believed that having a big ass would sort out how bad she felt about herself, how she hated her body and how she wanted to feel powerful. But that wasn't how the body, mind or behaviour worked.

I knew for a fact that Minty could have had the world's biggest ass and she never would have been happy and that was sad in a way.

But sometimes as a superhero you really couldn't save everyone, Minty was clearly one of them.

I put the paper in the small black waste bin by my desk and focused on the massive pile of folders on my desk because they were all the clients I was seeing today and these were the people that I could help, save and hopefully they wouldn't end up like Minty.

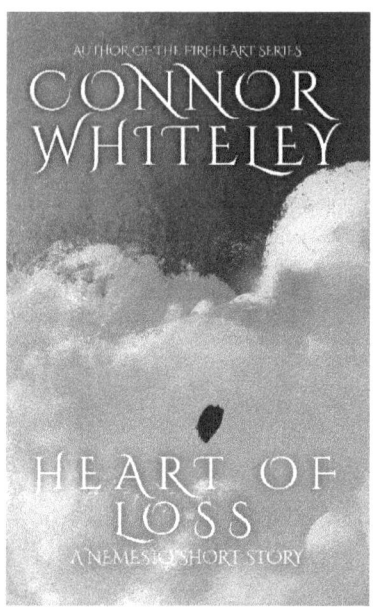

GET YOUR FREE AND EXCLUSIVE SHORT STORY
NOW! LEARN ABOUT NEMESIO'S PAST! And get
signed up to Connor Whiteley's newsletter to hear about new
gripping books, offers and exciting projects. (You'll never be
sent spam)

https://www.subscribepage.io/fireheart

## About The Author:

Connor Whiteley is the author of over 60 books in the sci-fi fantasy, nonfiction psychology and books for writer's genre and he is a Human Branding Speaker and Consultant.

He is a passionate warhammer 40,000 reader, psychology student and author.

Who narrates his own audiobooks and he hosts The Psychology World Podcast.

All whilst studying Psychology at the University of Kent, England.

Also, he was a former Explorer Scout where he gave a speech to the Maltese President in August 2018 and he attended Prince Charles' 70th Birthday Party at Buckingham Palace in May 2018.

Plus, he is a self-confessed coffee lover!

Other books by Connor Whiteley:

Love Betrays You

Lord of War Origin Trilogy:
Not Scared Of The Dark
Madness
Burn Them All

Way Of The Odyssey
Odyssey of Rebirth
Convergence of Odysseys

The Fireheart Fantasy Series
Heart of Fire
Heart of Lies
Heart of Prophecy
Heart of Bones
Heart of Fate

City of Assassins (Urban Fantasy)
City of Death
City of Martyrs
City of Pleasure
City of Power

Agents of The Emperor
Return of The Ancient Ones
Vigilance
Angels of Fire
Kingmaker
The Eight
The Lost Generation
Hunt

Emperor's Council
Speaker of Treachery
Birth Of The Empire
Terraforma
Spaceguard

The Rising Augusta Fantasy Adventure Series
Rise To Power
Rising Walls
Rising Force
Rising Realm

Lord Of War Trilogy (Agents of The Emperor)
Not Scared Of The Dark
Madness
Burn It All Down

Miscellaneous:
RETURN
FREEDOM
SALVATION
Reflection of Mount Flame
The Masked One
The Great Deer
English Independence

## OTHER SHORT STORIES BY CONNOR WHITELEY

Mystery Short Story Collections

Criminally Good Stories Volume 1: 20 Detective Mystery Short Stories

Criminally Good Stories Volume 2: 20 Private Investigator Short Stories

Criminally Good Stories Volume 3: 20 Crime Fiction Short Stories

Criminally Good Stories Volume 4: 20 Science Fiction and Fantasy Mystery Short Stories

Criminally Good Stories Volume 5: 20 Romantic Suspense Short Stories

Connor Whiteley Starter Collections:

Agents of The Emperor Starter Collection

Bettie English Starter Collection

Matilda Plum Starter Collection

Gay Romance Starter Collection

Way Of The Odyssey Starter Collection

Kendra Detective Fiction Starter Collection

Mystery Short Stories:

Protecting The Woman She Hated

Finding A Royal Friend

Our Woman In Paris

Corrupt Driving

A Prime Assassination

Jubilee Thief

Jubilee, Terror, Celebrations

Negative Jubilation

Ghostly Jubilation

Killing For Womenkind

A Snowy Death
Miracle Of Death
A Spy In Rome
The 12:30 To St Pancreas
A Country In Trouble
A Smokey Way To Go
A Spicy Way To Go
A Marketing Way To Go
A Missing Way To Go
A Showering Way To Go
Poison In The Candy Cane
Kendra Detective Mystery Collection Volume 1
Kendra Detective Mystery Collection Volume 2
Mystery Short Story Collection Volume 1
Mystery Short Story Collection Volume 2
Criminal Performance
Candy Detectives
Key To Birth In The Past

Science Fiction Short Stories:
Their Brave New World
Gummy Bear Detective
The Candy Detective
What Candies Fear
The Blurred Image
Shattered Legions
The First Rememberer
Life of A Rememberer
System of Wonder
Lifesaver
Remarkable Way She Died
The Interrogation of Annabella Stormic

Blade of The Emperor
Arbiter's Truth
Computation of Battle
Old One's Wrath
Puppets and Masters
Ship of Plague
Interrogation
Edge of Failure

Fantasy Short Stories:
City of Snow
City of Light
City of Vengeance
Dragons, Goats and Kingdom
Smog The Pathetic Dragon
Don't Go In The Shed
The Tomato Saver
The Remarkable Way She Died
Dragon Coins
Dragon Tea
Dragon Rider

All books in 'An Introductory Series':
Clinical Psychology and Transgender Clients
Clinical Psychology
Careers In Psychology
Psychology of Suicide
Dementia Psychology
Clinical Psychology Reflections Volume 4
Forensic Psychology of Terrorism And Hostage-Taking
Forensic Psychology of False Allegations
Year In Psychology
CBT For Anxiety
CBT For Depression
Applied Psychology
BIOLOGICAL PSYCHOLOGY 3RD EDITION
COGNITIVE PSYCHOLOGY THIRD EDITION
SOCIAL PSYCHOLOGY- 3RD EDITION
ABNORMAL PSYCHOLOGY 3RD EDITION
PSYCHOLOGY OF RELATIONSHIPS- 3RD EDITION
DEVELOPMENTAL PSYCHOLOGY 3RD EDITION
HEALTH PSYCHOLOGY
RESEARCH IN PSYCHOLOGY
A GUIDE TO MENTAL HEALTH AND TREATMENT
AROUND THE WORLD- A GLOBAL LOOK AT
DEPRESSION
FORENSIC PSYCHOLOGY
THE FORENSIC PSYCHOLOGY OF THEFT,
BURGLARY AND OTHER CRIMES AGAINST
PROPERTY
CRIMINAL PROFILING: A FORENSIC PSYCHOLOGY
GUIDE TO FBI PROFILING AND GEOGRAPHICAL
AND STATISTICAL PROFILING.
CLINICAL PSYCHOLOGY

Milton Keynes UK
Ingram Content Group UK Ltd.
UKHW050810010724
444982UK00015B/1171

9 781917 181075